Meely LaBauve

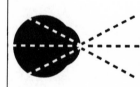 This Large Print Book carries the
Seal of Approval of N.A.V.H.

Meely LaBauve

Ken Wells

Thorndike Press • Thorndike, Maine

Published in 2001 by arrangement with Random House, Inc.

Thorndike Press Large Print Americana Series.

The tree indicium is a trademark of Thorndike Press.

The text of this Large Print edition is unabridged.
Other aspects of the book may vary from the original edition.

Set in 16 pt. Plantin.

Printed in the United States on permanent paper.

Library of Congress Cataloging-in-Publication Data

Wells, Ken.
    Meely LaBauve: a novel / Ken Wells.
      p. cm.
    ISBN 0-7862-3023-1 (lg. print : hc : alk. paper)
    1. Teenage boys — Fiction. 2. Alligator hunting — Fiction. 3. Fathers and sons — Fiction. 4. Louisiana — Fiction. 5. Cajuns — Fiction. 6. Large type books. I. Title.
PS3573.E4923 M44 2001
    813′.54—dc21   00-048000

IN MEMORY OF

BONNIE TOUPS WELLS,

MY MOTHER,

AND JERRY GORDON WELLS,

MY BROTHER:

GONE BUT NEVER FORGOTTEN.

ACKNOWLEDGMENTS

To my parents, who gave me what every child needs: love, encouragement, and a library card: to my father, Rex, particularly, for instilling in me his love of the wild lands of South Louisiana; to my late mother and my late Cajun grandmother Anna Virginia Toups, for passing on Cajun lore and their Cajun *joie de vivre;* to my late grandfather William Henry Wells, a character and gifted yarn-spinner if there ever was one; to Lora "Granny" Wells, who taught kindness by the very example of her life; to the Wells brothers — Bill, Pershing, Chris, and Bobby — creative spirits all and constant sources of inspiration; to early readers of this work, most notably my *Wall Street Journal* colleague (and bowling coach) Carrie Dolan, for her indispensable encouragement, and to Elizabeth Seay for her careful reading of the galleys; to Jim Sterba, another *WSJ* colleague, and my friend Fred Bob Burger in Anniston, Alabama, for their generous favors to Meely; to my mentor Al Delahaye at Nicholls State University in Thibodaux,

Louisiana, who taught me that 90 percent of writing is discipline and hard work; to my agent, the inestimable Timothy Seldes of Russell & Volkening, whose unwavering faith in Meely kept hope burning bright; to the indefatigable Joe Regal at R&V, who kept the devil out of the details; to the atomic bundle of talent and energy that is Lee Boudreaux, my Random House editor and my kindred Cajun spirit; her unflagging enthusiasm and keen eye made Meely not just possible but also a better book; to my daughters, Sara and Becca, the best audience a storytelling dad could ever have; to my wife, Lisa, for her long, long years of patience and encouragement in the wake of a writer's many ups and downs.

Lastly, to Cajuns in name and spirit everywhere.

Note: The first draft of this book was written aboard a New Jersey Transit train during my daily commute into Manhattan. The author acknowledges with grateful appreciation the hospitality of the NJT conductors and the consideration of Dr. Browning, friend and silent partner.

1

Daddy's gone off again to hunt gators. He says the police might come lookin' for him 'cause of some problem with his ole truck. He says I can hide or not.

I'm not gonna hide this time. If they come they'll ax me questions. But I won't know where Daddy is any more than they do. I'll say back in the swamp somewhere, which is close as I can come. They'll go lookin' but they won't find him, not unless he wants to be found. Or unless he gits drunk, which is always possible with Daddy, and he comes roarin' into town raisin' hell. He might run right into the police station and bust up a couple of 'em till they throw him in jail.

It sometimes happens that way. That's Daddy for you.

We live way down on the lonesome end of Catahoula Bayou. Our house is ugly and fallin' apart here and there. Daddy won't fix it. He says he's give up on houses and when this one falls down he won't have another. He'll go live in the woods.

He don't say what I'm s'posed to do.

When Momma was alive, she kept it up pretty well. She mopped and swept and got after Daddy to carpenter and paint and mow. He listened most times, as I remember.

But since Momma's gone, Daddy don't listen to nobody. He runs off into the swamps huntin' alligators and just stays. Otherwise, he's pretty much in town, drinkin' in a saloon.

I myself have never tried to tell Daddy anything, though I might one day.

My name is Emile LaBauve, Emile comin' from my Grandpa Toups on Momma's side. I never liked my name and people that know me, 'cept the teachers and Father Giroir, the bayou priest, call me Meely. I'm fifteen, small for my age everybody says. I tend to stay away from school and such. Every so often, the police come lookin' for me instead of Daddy. And I run off, too, and hide in the woods. It's amazin' how poor the police are at findin' people.

I hope I never git lost and need the police to find me for real.

The police come 'cause I live pretty well by myself and I don't go to school unless I want to. Daddy, him, he won't make me.

He says I'm pretty near growed and got his hound dog ways and Momma's brains. He says a hound dog is good at scroungin' and will never starve and somebody with brains can always figger out what to do.

He says I don't need much else, and anyway school never did him much good.

I don't mind school sometimes, just like sometimes I don't mind breakfast.

I wouldn't mind it, actually, if Daddy bought groceries now and then.

But I'm doin' okay. I've planted my own garden and there's fish and frogs and crawfish in the bayou and swamps, and I take my twenty-two out and shoot me some birds and rabbits and such.

Blackbirds is good, though people don't think so.

Heck, I roasted a mockin' bird in the oven once.

It cooked up itty-bitty but was all right. Sweet it was.

Junior Guidry says only a moron would shoot a mockin' bird 'cause the law is against such things and they could put you in the jailhouse. I don't say nothin' to Junior Guidry, usually, as I know he's plannin' to bust me up good one day. He's tried a few times already. Sometimes I look at him the way Daddy says I should, with the Evil Eye.

Junior's a big ole s.o.b. and mean as a gut-shot gator. He's been in eighth grade a long time. I keep hopin' he'll just quit school but he won't 'cause his momma makes him go.

Junior don't like the Evil Eye.

I don't know what the Evil Eye is all about. It comes from Daddy's side of the family. His ole Tante Eve knew all about it and put the *gris-gris* on lots of people and they took it serious. Daddy taught me how to look just like Tante Eve looked but it don't mean nothin' to me. But I guess I look like one scary booger when I do it.

That's what Daddy says.

Don't matter what it means, Meely, just what it looks like.

Junior thinks I'm crazy, which is prob'ly a good thing for Junior to think.

I got one real friend far as I know, Joey Hebert. He lives up the bayou in a big ole house kept nice. It's white and once, Joey says, slaves tended it. The yard's bigger than the grounds at school and the oak trees are so big and old that the slaves tended them, too. Mr. Hebert mows the grass hisself with a big tractor, though the Heberts, Joey says, got all the money in the world. His daddy could hire twenty people to cut the grass but he don't want to, Joey says. He just likes sittin' up on that tractor mowin' away. He don't work much any-more, otherwise.

The Heberts got all that cane land and people tend it and give Mr. Hebert the money. They got two Cadillacs, one black for Mr. Hebert and one white for Miz Hebert, and a pretty new red 1961 Ford pickup truck and a colored maid who dresses like a nurse, and a colored cook who does too.

Mr. Hebert mows the grass and drives his truck up and down the bayou lookin' at his cane land. He drives the Cadillac to church on Sundays.

He don't like me much, though Joey does.

Joey says I'm smart, which I think I am, and he says I'm lucky 'cause I git to do just what I want when I want to do it. He says he would love to skip school 'cept he cain't. He says I'm lucky I don't have a momma 'cause he has a momma and she gits on him every day about this or that. He says Daddy is a character and he wishes his daddy was. He says Daddy's right when he says a boy with hound dog ways and brains is about as good as a boy gits.

I agree with most of that and, anyway, Joey's the only person I know who's ever agreed with anything Daddy's said.

Me and Joey do things sometimes when he can slip away. We go swimmin' down at Poule D'eau Curve and I take him out in the woods and show him things I know about that Daddy's showed me. We catch garter snakes and frogs and we tease cottonmouths with willow switches, which ain't dangerous provided you use a pretty long switch. We track deer. We've never got close enough to shoot one, though we've seen the backsides of a few.

Once we shot a rabbit with my twenty-two. I skinned it and dabbed it with Tabasco sauce, which I carry in my huntin' vest, and we roasted it on a spit out in the woods over a fire I made. It was tender and good. We shot it out of huntin' season and Joey was afraid we'd git caught. But I laughed.

I told him I knew all about the police and game wardens, too. If they come to chase us, I knew just where to run.

Anyway, what do the police care if I eat me a rabbit?

Daddy says the woods and what's in 'em are free to a hungry man.

Joey says he agrees with this, too.

14

Joey is popular down at the school with the teachers and girls and such. He says he's gotta go to a college called Tulane — he cain't git out of it. His momma would have a fit 'cause her own daddy went there. He says he's gotta be a lawyer or else his Daddy will leave him out of his will. He says there's lots of money in that will, Meely, so you wouldn't wanna be left out of it.

After we ate that rabbit in the woods, he said he was gonna invite me to supper. But he ain't yet.

I'm interested in that big ole house. I think about slaves and ghosts and such.

And supper, sometimes.

2

It's Saturday mornin' and Chickie Naquin's come over. We're goin' crawfishin'. Chickie might be my only friend 'cept for Joey, though people up at school say Chickie ain't got no friends so maybe we're not friends after all.

Chickie don't always wash and he's fat though not as fat as some I've seen. He talks a lot and a shirt never got made that would stay tucked in his pants.

Daddy says the Naquins are like us — neither of us got a pot to pee in. Plus I ain't got a momma and Chickie ain't got a daddy, or much of a daddy, so that makes us pretty near even.

His daddy had a stroke and is a vegetable layin' around in a bed all day and night with his mouth open, people say.

A turnip is what Junior Guidry says is the kind of vegetable, which I know is a mean thing to say.

'Course, Chickie's momma's around lookin' after things as best she can.

I cain't usually say the same for Daddy.

I've got the crawfish bait — a bunch of fish guts that are nice and ripe, which is how crawfish like 'em — and a big bucket. Chickie's got a few ole crawfish nets, which he's slung over his shoulders. He claims he stole 'em from behind Elmore's Store up the bayou but the boy's been known to exaggerate.

Lookin' at Chickie's nets I'd say they was throwed away or give up on.

We walk out through the overgrowed backyard of our place and cut across a corner of a sugarcane field till we git to the Grassy Road. It's just a tractor path, wide enough for tractors goin' one way or another, but it winds for miles and miles through the fields before it skirts along the big oak ridge that rings Catahoula Swamp. Sugar's about all they grow around here but for a bit of corn in between, and some vegetables in narrow gardens along the bayou-side. Joey Hebert's daddy's got a lot of this cane.

The crawfish place I've got in mind is over on the backside of the oak ridge and it's a good walk — three miles I'd say. I've told Chickie this as I know he don't like walkin'. But he's promised not to complain long as we take it slow. Slow's fine with me — I got nothin' else to do.

It takes almost two hours to reach the edge of the woods and by this time Chickie's turned as red as a crab boiled in Zatarain's.

It'll be cooler in the shade of the woods I tell him.

He says I hope so, Meely. I'm sweatin' like a frog in a skillet.

I have to say I've seen lots of frogs up close but cain't recall 'em sweatin'. But I have seen fresh-skinned frogs jump out of the skillet if the grease is hot enough.

We've got to cross a log over a wide ditch between the cane field and the woods. I've done it a million times, even at night. Chickie looks at me and then the log and says what if I fall in that ditch?

I say it's a wide log, Chickie. Plus there ain't more'n two feet of water in that ditch. So if you fall in it ain't gonna kill you.

He says what about snakes?

I say you see any down there?

He says no, but they could be hidin' underwater.

I say snakes don't hide under the water. On a hot day like today they'll be out sunnin' on the banks or on a log. If there was snakes there you'd see 'em.

Chickie puzzles over this, then says well, Momma says they do hide underwater. She says them dirty cottonmouths will sneak up on you underwater and bite you and you'll drop dead on the spot. That's why she don't let me swim in the bayou. She tole me before I left this mornin', Chickie, cher, catch me some crawfish, yeah, but don't go git yourself bit, *neg*.

I say Chickie, no snake sneaks up on anybody and no snake 'round here kills you that quick. Daddy knew a man once who got bit by a water moccasin and walked five miles to town to the hospital. They give him a shot of this or that and fixed him up in a few days. Anyways, ain't no snakes down there. C'mon, I'll go across first. Gimme your nets.

Chickie hands 'em to me. He says well, Momma won't like it if I come back dead.

I gotta laugh at this.

I say well, if you git killed by a snake and die on me I just won't bring you back.

Meely! You'd leave me out here in these woods to rot? Like a *chaoui* on the side of the road?

I say Chickie, I'm jokin'.

Chickie looks at me about to pout then decides a grin is better. People tease Chickie a lot but nobody jokes with him much. There's a difference and I can tell he ain't used to it.

Chickie says okay. You go first.

I skip across the log. Chickie gits on and takes a few baby steps and starts flappin' his arms like a wrung-neck chicken and then falls off.

It's only about a five-foot fall and he lands on his behind. He's flailin' around with his arms, churnin' up mud like an alligator in *flottant*.

I've got knee-high rubber boots and, though they leak some, I wade down into the ditch and help him up. We slip-slide up the bank and Chickie makes it to the top huffin' and puffin' and sits down.

He says I've ruint my shoes, Meely. Momma's gonna kill me. Kill me! I've ruint everything.

I'd noticed Chickie's shoes back at the house. They're black sneakers with white rubber round the bottom. The right one has a fair-sized hole in the toe. In my opinion they were pretty close to ruint already. My shoes back at the house ain't much better.

I say Chickie, it's just mud and mud ain't never killed nobody. If it did, I'd be dead long ago. When we git over to the crawfish spot we'll wash 'em off.

He says what about my pants and shirt?

I say same thing.

Chickie's a bit of trouble but he ain't dumb as most people think. And he ain't mean, which is a lot not to be.

We hike on through the woods and it's an easy hike if you stay out of the palmetto brakes. There's a few stray cows that run in here — some of 'em might be Mr. Hebert's as he's got cattle, too — and they keep the brush down pretty good. It's mostly live oak with Spanish moss and ash and hackberry and palmetto and jack vine and some muscadine, with Tupelo gum and cypress where the land gits low. It's beautiful in here — Daddy thinks so, too — though I've never been in woods, 'cept maybe scrub willow, that wasn't.

We git to the crawfish spot where the ridge gives up to water. The swamp's shallow here and there's woods irises bloomin' deep blue along the bank and cypress knees pokin' up everywhere. A fox squirrel goes skitterin' up an oak and is gone as quick as we saw him and a woodpecker knocks loud on a cypress not far off and it echoes between the trees.

Then the woods gets still. Not a breath of wind.

I put down the bucket and the nets and tell Chickie to go rummage around and find us a nice big stick, maybe four or five foot long. I grab a handful of fish guts and bait the first net, usin' twine to hold the bait on, then bait the others, then dabble my hands in swamp water to clean 'em off. These nets are small and held on four corners by coat hanger wire crossed at the top. You put 'em out and leave 'em sit for fifteen or twenty minutes. If there's crawfish about they'll swarm to the bait. You lift the net quick with the stick and pour your crawfish in the bucket before they scramble out the net. Caught crawfish are pretty quick when they want to git away, even though they do skitter backward.

Chickie comes back with a good-lookin' stick — a stout branch from a cypress tree, pointy on one end where it broke off.

He says Meely, what would you do if you didn't have these nets?

I say make a puh-lonk like Daddy showed me.

He says what's a *puh-lonk?*

I say a puh-lonk is just a stretch of twine six or seven feet long. You tie your bait to one end, hold on to the other end, and throw it in the water. When it hits the water, it goes *puh-lonk.*

Chickie laughs at this. I did, too, the first time Daddy called it that.

We put out our nets and wait, then I go

with Chickie over to a place about thirty or forty yards down the bank where there's a little pool, maybe three foot around, that's just deep enough to jump in. There's a nice big stump on the edge makin' it easy to git in and out. On hot days, I've used the pool to cool off, though it ain't deep or wide enough to swim in. People think swamp water is dirty and some of it is. But there's a little slough comin' way over from the Catahoula Marsh that flows in here and keeps this water sweet.

I shuck my boots and strip down to my drawers and jump in the pool to prove to Chickie there ain't no snakes down there. I git out and after a bit of coaxin' he jumps in with everything on.

Chickie ducks his head underwater to git the mud out of his hair then splashes around. He climbs out after about ten minutes lookin' like a dog left out in the rain. But at least the mud's gone. I hand him my T-shirt to dry his face and we walk back down to our nets.

And doggone it if every one of 'em ain't loaded with big red swamp crawfish.

Chickie ain't done much crawfishin' in his life or spent any real time in the woods and he squeals happy as a slopped hog every time I raise a net.

He says Meely, look at these crawdads! These are bigger'n the ones my Uncle Theophile catches in Belle River.

He might be right, and I cain't say I've caught any that were better. In about an hour we've got the bucket three quarters full, which is about as many crawfish as I wanna carry back, considerin' how far we have to walk.

While we're doin' this, Chickie's apparently forgot about his ruint shoes 'cause every time some mudbug scoots over the side of a net, as one or two always do every time we lift it, Chickie runs in the water to catch it 'fore it gits away. He grabs one of those real big boys and it grabs him back on the finger — big crawfish have big claws. Chickie gives a yell — Ai, yi, yi! — and throws up his arm and flings that crawfish clear up to a cypress branch where it lands in a ball of moss.

It sticks.

We look up and there's that crawdad wavin' its big red claws at us about twenty foot above the ground and we bust out laughin'. A squirrel or a crow or a woodpecker will come along pretty soon and be puzzled by this. If a coon comes, he'll git a free meal.

I tell Chickie it's time to head back and I

24

also tell him he ought to at least roll up his pants so he don't git 'em all muddied again. He does and we gather up our crawfish and nets and go. Chickie keeps the stick, which he uses to poke at the ground here and there.

I decide to go back a different way, followin' the swamp bank to where the slough comes in, then cut across the ridge back to the ditch. It's maybe a half mile out of the way but there's some big cypress trees in there that I think Chickie would like to see. Daddy calls 'em the Church Trees 'cause if you stand right under 'em and look up, they look like they go clear to heaven.

We walk about a quarter mile and come upon a sorry sight — a brown-and-white drowned cow about twenty yards out in the swamp. Poor thing prob'ly stepped in a hole and bogged down and drowned, or couldn't git out and starved.

This is one of the dangers of walkin' swamp. Even in the shallow water you never know if the bottom'll be there on the next step.

The cow's been here for several days as it's all blowed up and stinkin'. I pinch my nose but Chickie don't. He's never seen a drowned cow or one swole up so big.

Before I know it, Chickie's wadin' out toward the cow. I don't think much of this idea.

I say Chickie, whatcha doin'?

He says just lookin', Meely.

Well you can see that cow good from here. Plus you better be careful. There's prob'ly a deep hole out there. That's why that cow got bogged down.

He says I'm walkin' slow. I just wanna see better.

Chickie is pretty soon at that cow in knee-deep water.

He says watch this, Meely.

He raises his stick over his head with both hands, the sharp end of it pointin' down.

I yell no, Chickie! NO!!!

Too late.

Chickie stabs the cow's belly hard with the stick and it explodes like a hunderd mules fartin' green clover.

There's a shower of cow matter and Chickie's knocked down backward and the smell is so awful that I'm just about knocked down too.

I drop the crawfish bucket and the nets and put my left hand over my mouth and nose and rush in the water to Chickie.

I've never seen such a mess of a human

being. He's half sittin' up in swamp goo and his face, hair, and shirt are covered with cow blow and white squirmy things.

I say Lord, Chickie. Lord.

I'm blinded! Chickie howls. I'm blinded, Meely!

I look close. Chickie's actually got his eyes shut tight so I strip off my T-shirt again and wipe his eyes and his face.

I say now look up here at me, Chickie.

He opens his eyes.

I say can you see me?

He says yeah.

So you're not blind, okay?

Okay.

I say you are a mess though.

Chickie looks down at his shirt and then his arms.

Them maggots, Meely?

I say well, somethin' like that.

Meely, Momma says maggots eat out your brains.

Only if you're dead, Chickie. You ain't dead, okay?

Chickie starts to shiver and rake at his arms. He says git 'em off of me, Meely. Please!

Then he says I think I'm gonna throw up.

I think I might, too.

I go round behind and git my arms around his chest and drag him to the bank. I git the crawfish bucket and, though I hate to do this, I dump 'em out on a spot of high ground as far from the water as I can manage. Then I wade into a part of the swamp that Chickie hasn't muddied and dip up a bucketful of water.

I have Chickie kneel down and I douse him.

Six or seven buckets later Chickie's back to lookin' like a half-drowned muskrat, which is an improvement.

I then run over to where I dumped the crawdads and start roundin' 'em up one at a time. Crawfish are slow on land and I knew most of them wouldn't git very far. Chickie comes over to help, though he don't git many 'cause he's scared of bein' pinched again. Though they've scattered everywhere we git most of them back in the bucket.

Chickie looks at me sheepish.

He says do you think I'm stupid, Meely?

I say no.

He says but that was a stupid thing to do, right?

I say yeah. But listen', Chickie, we all do stupid things sometimes. Now you know better.

Chickie shakes his head. He says I didn't know a cow could blow up like that. Did you?

I'm tempted to be cross at Chickie but it's a hard thing to do.

I say no, that's a new one in my book, too.

Chickie looks at me with that grin again.

He says you won't tell, will you?

Tell who?

Kids at school. 'Specially that Junior. You know how he gits on me.

I say no, I won't tell Junior.

He says whew.

I say I might tell your momma though.

Meely!

I say Chickie, it's okay. I'm jokin' again. Really.

He says don't tell Momma. She'll kill me.

I say she prob'ly would. Me too.

Chickie pops out laughin' at that. Boy, she would, wouldn't she? Murder us both, Meely.

We make our way out of the woods and Chickie makes it across the log this time without fallin' in. We hike back to my house and there's a truck pulled up in the driveway. It's Chickie's Uncle Theophile.

By this time we've dried off and Chickie don't look no worse than usual. I tell him to take all the crawfish and he says no,

29

Meely, we'll split 'em or at least why don't you come over and Momma will boil 'em for us. She's got some Zatarain's.

But I'm tired and, anyways, the way I eat crawfish I wouldn't but git started and we'd be done. Plus Miz Naquin's an excitable woman and who knows what Chickie himself might blurt out about that cow. Then I'd never hear the end of it.

Never.

Chickie's Uncle Theophile ain't never got much to say, at least to me, but he does say boys, y'all caught some nice-lookin' crawdads, I gotta hand it to you.

They drive off and I go in to see if maybe Daddy's come home. But the ole Dodge ain't here so I s'pect he's not. I go round the back of the house, past the cypress cistern, and go cloppin' up the back porch steps and through the kitchen door. The house ain't locked. It never is. Daddy says people who ain't got a pot to pee in ain't got nothin' worth stealin'. It's dark inside 'cept where a streak of sun comes in the kitchen window.

I go peek in Daddy's room 'cause sometimes his truck breaks down and he thumbs a ride home. But his room is as empty and lonesome as a church on Tuesday.

3

It's Monday and Daddy still ain't back, which don't really surprise me, and I decide to go up to school. Miz Breaux, the principal, don't like it much when I show up right out of the blue. But she lets me in after she fusses me. She don't spank me no more, though she used to.

She still spanks Junior Guidry and that bunch when they misbehave, which is okay by me. They laugh afterward, but I know it hurts.

Miz Breaux's little but she swings big, like a man.

Up at Catahoula School we've got all the grades. I'm in ninth when I'm in anything. My teacher is Miz Henrietta Lirette, who's nice as pie. She don't even scold me no more. She says I write good even though I don't spell right, which I know is true. She says if I put my mind to it, I could be a good student. I don't mind history and even science but 'rithmetic makes my head hurt. I've had a look at algebra and I cain't make heads or tails of it. I can figger enough already so that when I go up the bayou to Elmore's Store to git a *pop rouge*, I never git gypped. I cain't imagine havin' to figger anything so hard that I'd need algebra to figger it.

I like school in the mornin' when the kids play softball before classes. I don't have a glove but I borrow Joey's, who's got two. I play shortstop and I'm fast as a strikin' cottonmouth. I play on Joey's team and we always lose 'cause Junior Guidry and his bunch always play together.

They're mostly big and slow but Junior himself can hit a ball a country mile.

I'm sorry he can, and I hate to admit he can. But it's true.

But if he ever hits it to shortstop, he's out. I throw him out every time and he throws a tantrum, which I like to see. One time he come after me but Miz Lirette was watchin' and she jumped on him faster than a rooster jumps a hen. He got hauled in to see Miz Breaux, who whupped his butt good.

I was tickled.

What's really best about school is that they serve dinner and I git to eat regular food. We've got a nice cafeteria and two colored cooks. They make a lot of red beans and rice and dirty rice, too, which is fine with me. Momma used to cook both. Dinner only costs thirty-five cents and Joey pays for me the times I don't have money, which is usual. Sometimes the fat cook, Ella Mae, gives me extra.

I like Ella Mae. She laughs big as Christmas.

I once ate at Miz Lirette's house. She invited me over. Daddy, too, but Daddy wouldn't go. Daddy ain't a goer.

Miz Lirette even come to pick me up in her car. She lives in a nice house give to her by her daddy and momma who died years ago. He used to be a cane man, too, though not as big as Mr. Hebert. Her house is big, the ceilings go up and up, and there's a staircase that looks like it come out of a movie.

Miz Lirette ain't married, though kids at school say she was s'posed to be married once to a man who moved away. She lives in that house with her older sister who was married but her husband died. They have a dinin' room with a big table that's got lion's paws carved into the legs.

That's where we ate. It was set with a red-and-white checkered tablecloth. Miz Lirette had cooked a gumbo and snap beans and a jambalaya, too. She served homemade root beer to drink. She showed me how to hold my fork and spoon proper, which I know Momma had tried to do but I was only six or seven when she done it. I ate and ate and ate.

I drunk a whole tub of root beer, which made Miz Lirette chuckle.

She reminds me a bit of Momma, what I remember of her.

Sometimes at school I hang around with Chickie. Junior and that bunch pick on Chickie like they sometimes pick on me. When they see us together, they hold their noses and make pig noises or some such. They call him Fat Ass and Fart Face or things that are worse. Names don't bother me, 'cause I know I always got the Evil Eye. I know they bother Chickie, though.

Not long ago Chickie told me about girls. He said if you go over to the wooden bleachers up by the softball field at recess, you can see Mary Portier sittin' on the top step every day. He said Mary sits there readin' books and don't sit proper. Most days you can see her drawers.

He said she seems to wear yellow a lot.

He said do you know what's under her drawers?

I said well, I guess so.

He said well, you must not if you guess so.

He said heaven is under there.

I said I guess I knew that.

He said Junior Guidry and that bunch know all about heaven, maybe Joey, too. He said Bertha Bonvillain, the pimply girl with the big titties in eleventh grade, goes with Junior and a bunch of boys back of Eustus Daigle's barn in the cane field. He said Bertha shows all them boys her drawers, then she takes 'em off and they all root around together. In heaven.

It don't seem possible to me. But I guess it could be so.

Chickie thinks maybe Joey and Claudia Toups, the prettiest girl at Catahoula School, go to heaven, too. But he said they don't have to go rootin' around in the cane field like hogs, since Joey's got such a big house. He says they just go in there and hide and do stuff.

I wonder about that. I think I know maybe what it is they do. I think I've got a pretty good idea. But maybe I don't.

Momma never told me about such 'cause I was little, I guess. And when I axed Daddy once, he threw his head back and cawed like a crow.

He said that's one thing you'll figger out

for yourself, Meely. For shore, son!

Daddy figgers I'll figger out everything sooner or later.

I hardly know any of the girls at school. Claudia Toups is s'posed to be a distant cousin on my Grandma Toups's side but she don't pay me no mind. Daddy says the whole family got no use for us 'cause we're swamp rats, which I guess we are, and got the Wild Injun in us, which I guess we do. Still, I like to look at Claudia from a distance, even if she don't look back at me.

I don't mind girls, though I guess I might be scared of 'em.

At the end of school, I find Chickie and I say let's go look at Mary Portier.

We go over to the bleachers but Mary's not there.

4

After school, I walk up to Mandalay Plantation, where lots of the colored field hands live. The coloreds do all the real work there is to be done in sugar, far as I can tell. I have a cane pole and a can of worms. I'm gonna go fish a place I call the Perch Hole up in a deep bend of Catahoula Bayou.

There's lots of good fishin' holes on Catahoula Bayou — there's eleven miles of water between here and town and five more 'tween us and Bayou Go-to-Hell, which comes out of Catahoula Swamp. But I like the Perch Hole 'cause when I ain't got a boat, which is most of the time, it's not that far to walk to and it's easy fishin' from the bank. Usually Daddy's got the pirogue huntin' gators, but if he's left it, I'll take it out and paddle way up the bayou toward town, five or six miles, to a place called Cypress Bend where Catahoula makes a long, lazy curve. There's a little *traînasse* comin' out of a sweet-water marsh there where some big bass hang out. I've caught some three or four pounds. There's also a deep *sac-à-lait* hole, and if you catch 'em schoolin' in the spring and you've got enough grass shrimp, you could sink a pirogue with 'em. I never catch more than I need, though, as Daddy says it ain't right.

I pass a bayouside garden and there's a colored girl there with a hoe. Seems to me I used to see her a lot but I cain't recall seein' her much lately. She's lanky and barefooted and has on a wore-out flowery dress. Her hair is done in pigtails. She's choppin' Johnson grass, which I know is hot work in the sun 'cause I do it sometimes. Roots of that doggone Johnson grass grow pretty near down to China.

She stops choppin' when she sees me.

She says you Meely LaBauve, I bet.

I say I might be.

Your daddy's that crazy white man, I bet.

I say some would say that's him.

She says he hunts gators, don't he?

I say he does.

She says them gators ever bite him?

I say not yet.

She throws her head back and squawks like a chicken.

She says before my daddy passed, he wouldn't go nowhere near the swamps.

Scared of gators and moccasins and the *loup garou.*

I say Daddy hunts snakes, too.

He kills 'em, you mean?

I say, no, he c'lecks 'em live, for zoos and such.

C'lecks 'em? Like butterflies?

Kinda like that.

She says cottonmouths, too?

I say any kind, don't matter to Daddy. Don't matter to me, neither.

She says you catch them nasty ole snakes, too?

Well, I'm like Daddy, I catch about everything. If us LaBauves don't catch, we don't eat.

She says well, ain't you somethin', Meely. She smiles so hard that her eyes crinkle up like day-old biscuits.

She says what kind of name is Meely? You related to corn or somethin'?

She laughs big again.

I gotta smile at this myself.

I say no. Emile is what Momma named me but I never took to it.

Hhhm. Emile's okay but Meely's nice. I like it.

I nod.

She says I know your daddy catches them coons 'cause he comes round here sellin' 'em for a dollar. We've bought lots from him. Momma loves to barbecue coons.

I say I've eat 'em, too, though not barbecued. My momma used to stew 'em, what I remember.

She says you catch them coons, too?

I say shore.

She says trap 'em or hunt 'em?

I say a bit of both.

She says you ever caught you a colored girl?

I'm puzzled at this.

I say what you mean, in a trap?

She busts out laughin' again. She says you're a funny boy, you know that?

I say I reckon I could be.

She says by the way, my name is Cassie, Cassie Jackson.

I say I know who you are from a while ago. But I cain't say I've seen you much lately.

She says .well, I'd been stayin' with an aunt over on the edge of town. She'd been sick for quite a while and Momma wanted me to help out. Her mister died and she had but one boy of her own and he moved far away in the army. She passed, too. Not that long ago.

I say I'm sorry to hear that.

She says, well, she was ole. Ten years older than Momma.

We go silent for a while.

Then I ax does she wanna go fishin' as I have to go. Supper and such as that.

She laughs real loud at that.

She says now Meely, what would happen out here on this bayou if a white boy and colored gal got caught fishin' together?

I say I dunno. What?

She says haw! You don't know nothin', do you, Meely LaBauve?

But she don't say it bad so I don't take it wrong.

I say well, maybe I know a coupla things. I shrug and go off fishin'.

5

I catch a whole mess of fish, mostly goggle-eye with a *sac-à-lait* or two thrown in. The Perch Hole is a pretty spot and I can sit under a mossy oak tree and stay cool, even in the hottest part of the day. The water's clear and black as tea and there's a stand of willow and hackberry across on the other bank, with a good-sized cypress in the middle, its knees pokin' up from the water's edge. There's a fella way down the swamp end of the bayou that saws off them knees and makes lamps out of 'em, which he sells to town people for good money.

Daddy don't approve of such. He says them knees is the root of the tree and a tree without roots won't be a tree much longer.

There's a great blue heron that stays over on the far bank near that cypress, huntin' minnows in the shallows. I see him pretty much every time I'm here. He used to fly away but he don't no more.

Curious bird he is, walkin' slow as winter on them stilt legs till he sees somethin', then peckin' like lightnin'. I'm glad I'm not a minnow.

The other reason I like fishin' the Perch Hole is that there ain't no *choupique* in here. Don't git me wrong — *choupique*'s the best fightin' fish there is in these waters. But I won't eat 'em normally 'cause they're seriously ugly and they taste like the swamp, though if I'm hungry enough I'll eat whatever there is.

As Daddy says, a hungry man ain't normally a picky man.

A lot of the ole Cajuns like *choupique,* though. They'll grind 'em up into meatballs. Some people figger that with enough cayenne, bay leaf, and shallots, you could eat ground-up mule. And I guess you could.

Daddy don't like to eat *choupique,* either, 'less he's desperate, but for another reason. He says *choupique* are like dinosaurs. They've been around about as long as the bayou itself, and somethin' so old shouldn't be messed with.

Daddy has peculiar notions.

Back home, I fry up the fish in a skillet, and some potatoes, too, though my potatoes are gittin' a little rugged, as they've started to sprout from the eyes. Chickie Naquin says boys ain't s'posed to cook but most boys don't have to, I guess. I don't really mind. Daddy cooks, too, sometimes.

It's one of the things he ain't give up on yet.

We don't have lights in our house 'cause Daddy ran outta money and says, anyway, he don't believe in lights no more, same as he don't believe in houses. So I eat supper out on the back porch by a candle if the mosquitoes ain't bad. Otherwise I sit at our rickety table and look out the window and watch lightnin' bugs out in the yard. On real dark nights you can see millions of 'em.

I wouldn't mind if the icebox worked. I'd like a glass of cold water now and then. I'd complain to Daddy if I thought it would do any good.

After supper, I take my huntin' light, which we call a bulleye and strap it around my head and git my twenty-two and go off walkin' down the Grassy Road toward the woods, shinin' rabbits. It ain't rabbit season, and you gotta be careful about rabbit fever. Daddy had it once and he shook like he had malaria for three days. He says it's the worst thing he ever got.

I skin spring rabbits careful and if I find the worms that give you the fever, I throw the rabbit away. I wash my hands real careful.

I gotta watch out for the game wardens, too, but they don't come out here much no more. They're too busy lookin' for Daddy in the deep swamp. They would love to catch him bulleyein' deer.

The cane's not too high yet and the kill-deer sit on the dirt road where they nestle into the Johnson grass and clover and soak up the warmth from the ground. You hit 'em with the bulleye and their eyes turn red, like big shiny marbles. Whippoorwills call out from the fallows, makin' a lonesome sound.

I spy a rabbit at the edge of a borrow ditch. Funny thing about shinin' a light in critters' eyes. They just sit there, still as the moon.

I cock the rifle, square up the light over the sights, and shoot.

I shoot good, Daddy says.

I do this time, for shore. The rabbit plops over.

I pick him up and throw him in my huntin' vest. I kill one more before I git to the woods. Two's about all I can eat before they go bad.

I leave the Grassy Road and cut through a cornfield, goin' the opposite way from where Chickie and I went crawfishin'. I cross over a rickety bridge and into the woods. Tractors used to come over this bridge, but it's wore out now. There was an ole farm back in a clearing here once, but it's long been gone. I hike up a ways along a little manmade canal. At the end of it sits Dead John's, a place Daddy's showed me.

Daddy's taught me all about the night woods. Used to, we'd hunt coons a lot together but we don't much lately. Sometimes we'd walk most of the night, pickin' up a coon here and there. But it didn't matter much how many coons we got. Daddy likes nighttime rambles. Sometimes we'd spy a deer or an otter or come upon a bunch of flyin' squirrels chatterin' as they sailed from tree to tree ahead of our lights. You'd never know what you might run across.

That's why I don't believe in the *loup garou*. If that ole wolfman lived in these deep night woods, Daddy and me would've found him.

Daddy says these woods go a long way to a swamp so big it would take two days to cross it in a pirogue. He himself has never got all the way across it. He says there used to be cypress in that swamp so big that you could stand in a grove all day and not once get to see the sun 'cause them trees blocked it out. He says all them giant trees got sawed down about fifty years ago, which is a shame since the men who cut 'em could have left a few for people to see now. He says there's still stumps back there as big around as a cistern.

In a bit I git to Dead John's. It's an ole colored graveyard, set in a clearin' that the woods have pretty well growed over. Joey Hebert says he's comin' here with me one night when he gits up the nerve. I ain't never been scared out in the woods at night, even here. I ain't superstitious.

I figger the dead's dead, like Momma, and if I ever see a ghost that wouldn't be so bad 'cause maybe it means I could see Momma, too.

But Daddy says the dead can only hurt you once, and I believe that's true.

I find it peaceful out here. You can look up through the ring of trees and see a million stars shinin' in the black sky. I find it comfortin' that the sky is so crowded with stars.

Coloreds bury their dead just like Cajuns do, in little cement tombs above ground. Keeps 'em out of the wet and away from the worms, I reckon.

I lay down on Dead John's tomb itself — at least the one everybody says is his. I look up at the stars and see the full moon in the sky. I see a shootin' star, a thin red thread on the black sky.

I lay there for a good bit, dozin' on and off, till the mosquitoes buzz out of the slough and find me, then head home.

I walk with my light off most of the way, lettin' the stars and moon light the way.

6

Daddy's come home.

He's sittin' in the livin' room on the saggy green couch with a woman. He's got a lamp goin'. He's liquored up some, but not yet drunk. I know the difference.

He says hello, Meely, bulleyein' rabbits?

Yes, got two.

This is Velma. Met her up up in Yankee City.

I say hello.

She says hello back.

I look at her careful.

She's blond, hair piled up high. She's got a cigarette danglin' in her mouth. I'd say she's a saloon girl, what I know of such things.

I say any gators, Daddy?

He says four fair-sized ones. I already skinned 'em and c'leckted the money.

I say that's good.

He says tomorrow I'm buyin' groceries.

I say that'll be real good.

Velma says Logan, your boy's perty. Small but perty.

She talks twangy, like people I've heard who are from Texas.

Daddy laughs at this. He says that boy's gator-tough. He's a runt but he's got hound dog ways, and brains to boot.

Velma laughs. When she does, I see she's got one tooth missin'. Daddy's missin' a few hisself.

I say I gotta go skin these rabbits.

Daddy says it seems a little late for skinnin' rabbits, son.

I say well, I got to, else they'll spoil.

Daddy says sorry we ain't got a porch light.

I say I don't care that much for lights, Daddy. Lamps work okay.

He says I'll buy some tomato sauce and fixins and I'll cook rabbit *sauce piquante.*

That sounds good to me, Daddy.

Velma says Logan, you never told me you could cook.

Shuh, Daddy says. Me and Meely, us, we can cook us up a storm.

She says is that right, Meely?

I say yes ma'am, it's right.

I git a kerosene lamp down from a shelf in the kitchen and go out to the skinnin' shed. Rabbits is the easiest thing there is to skin. Cut the fur at the belly and clear round the back and just pull it off. It don't take me no time. I gut 'em and throw the guts out on the edge of the field. A mink or possum or coon'll come along sometime tonight and eat 'em.

And if the critters don't get 'em, the chickens will in the mornin'.

People would be surprised what chickens eat.

I always am.

I go back in the house. I'm tired as a wore-out tractor. I'm thinkin' 'bout goin' to school again tomorrow. I guess sometimes I don't mind the company.

Velma and Daddy are nowhere to be seen. I hear 'em laughin' in Daddy's bedroom. I hear 'em carryin' on.

They sound pretty well drunk now.

I wash my hands and face at the kitchen sink. I go to the bathroom and pee and then go to my little room and shut the door. I don't bother takin' off my clothes. I flop on the bed and listen to Daddy and Velma carryin' on in the bedroom.

I wonder if Daddy's gonna git to heaven tonight.

Knowin' Daddy, I figger he will.

I shut my eyes and drift off to sleep.

Next thing I know, there's hollerin'.

I jump up and go see.

Velma's hollerin', so is Daddy.

She's caught the bed on fire with her cigarette. Smoke's pourin' out everywhere.

She runs out of the bedroom plumb naked, Daddy right after her, naked, too. The moon's now up high and shinin' bright in the window.

Velma don't look too bad. A little saggy is all.

I run to the kitchen and grab the mop bucket. I fill it at the sink and run back in.

Daddy meets me in the hall and says gimme that, son.

I hand it over.

He runs back in the room and throws the water on the bed.

Two or three more times and we've got it licked.

Me and Daddy grab the mattress and drag it outside into the yard. It smells like burnt feathers.

Back inside Velma says she's sorry. She's standin' in the hall, her shirt pulled around her. There's still lots to see, which I guess I don't mind.

Velma says oh God, Logan, I'm terrible sorry.

Daddy says don't worry, Velma, 'cause you know, I'm about through with beds anyway. We'll sleep on the sofa.

Daddy tousles my head and says my boy

thinks fast don't he?

Velma says he shore does.

I don't say nothin'. I'm just glad the house ain't burnt down as I ain't give up on houses just yet. Beds either.

Daddy still don't bother with clothes. He goes into the room and finds the bottle they was workin' on. He comes out and he and Velma trade it back and forth and giggle away.

Daddy holds the bottle out to me but I shake my head.

I go back into my room and shut the door.

But I cain't sleep.

I wish Chickie Naquin hadn't talked about girls like that.

I think about Velma and her pale skin and those smooth parts that were showin'.

I think about Mary Portier up on the bleacher steps, sittin' improper.

I think about Cassie Jackson and her long black legs.

I think about heaven.

7

In the mornin', Velma wakes me up.

She says do you want some breakfast, Meely?

I say please, thank you.

She says I've cooked up some grits. There's no milk or butter but I've found some brown sugar.

I say that would be fine.

She says do you drink coffee?

I say yes ma'am, I do.

Well, I'll fix some, too, though I hope you drink it black.

I say I've learned to since Daddy give up on electricity.

Velma laughs.

She says your daddy's got up early and has gone to the store like he promised.

I say I'm glad to hear that. Them rabbits won't keep very long.

In the daylight Velma's face is puffy and there's small dark bags under her eyes. She's got on green stretchy pants and a shiny red blouse. She looks wore out to me — not old necessarily, but tired out.

Paddled hard and put up wet, Daddy would say.

She looked better naked in the moonlight, but I guess anybody might.

She goes off to the kitchen. I go into the bathroom and pee and splash a little water on my face. I drag a comb through my hair but it don't do much good. I've got a fearsome cowlick.

I follow after Velma into the kitchen.

She's at the stove stirrin' the grits. The coffee's been put to drip — Community Coffee with chicory is what we drink — and it smells good. It's the friendliest smell in the world, far as I'm concerned.

Velma turns and sees me and smiles.

She says grits are about done. Coffee, too. I'll guess you like it strong like your daddy does.

I say yes ma'am, I do.

I take a seat at the table.

She says Meely, what do you do when your daddy's not here?

I say whatever comes to mind. I hunt and fish mostly.

What do you do about food?

Hunt and fish mostly.

She says what about school?

I say I go sometimes.

She says do you mind if I ask you what

happened to your momma?

Didn't Daddy tell you?

No, he didn't.

I say Momma died havin' a baby.

She says oh, I'm so sorry. What happened to the baby?

Died too.

Long ago?

I was seven.

She says do you like bein' alone here in this ole house?

I say it's okay most times.

Velma takes out a cigarette and lights it with a match. She inhales and blows smoke out of her nose. She says your daddy's somethin' else.

I say I s'pect he is.

She says he shore does think well of you.

I say well, I'm glad of that.

She says I've got me a girl of my own. A little girl only six. Did your daddy tell you that?

No ma'am.

Velma drags on her cigarette again.

She says well I guess he wouldn't. He don't really know me so well.

No ma'am.

She says my little girl lives with her daddy back where I come from. We ain't together no more, him and me. Ain't been for a while.

I say no ma'am.

She says I miss that girl.

I say yes ma'am.

Velma takes another drag of her cigarette. Things go quiet for a while. Velma goes to the stove and stirs the grits once more, then turns off the fire. She brings the pot to the table and dishes out the grits, some for me and some for her. They're done just right.

She puts the pot back on the stove and brings the coffeepot and puts it down on a towel she's folded up on the table. She pours for both of us and then sits down.

The grits are good. I eat a bowlful and Velma jumps up to dish me out some more. I ain't used to bein' waited on. She sits back down and eats slow and sips her coffee the same way. She takes another drag on her cigarette and then snubs it out in a jar lid that's sittin' on the table.

She says boy was that a night.

I say it shore was, Velma.

She says I hope your daddy ain't gonna hold that mattress against me.

I say don't worry. I think Daddy's done give up on mattresses. I'll bet he's prob'ly done forgot about it.

She says you were really thinkin' on your feet.

I say it's a good thing to do around here.

She laughs.

Velma pours herself some more coffee and me, too.

She says well, I got somethin' I wanna give you.

I say what could that be?

She says you just wait here a minute.

Velma gits up from the table and goes down the hall to the livin' room and comes back with her purse. She opens it up and takes out a wad of money.

She says take this.

I say for what?

Well, your daddy give it to me last night. To hold.

Well, why don't you give it back to Daddy?

She says well, I'll bet he's forgot. And I thought maybe you could use it.

I don't quite know what to say. A little money wouldn't be so bad.

For a rainy day, Velma says.

I say are you shore?

She says I'm shore, Meely.

Velma hands me the money.

I git up on my tippytoes and git down an empty coffee can from way back in the cupboard and put it in there, then put the can back.

I go back to my coffee and grits.

Daddy comes home pretty soon. He's in a good mood. He's got a load of groceries, the first in a while. He's got lots of pork 'n' beans and a big sack of red beans and a big sack of rice. He's got lots of tomato sauce and some Tabasco and celery and onions and hot peppers to make our *sauce piquante.* He's bought a block of ice for that dented ice chest on the porch and has brought home some milk and eggs, though the milk will have to be drunk quick.

Velma says Logan, I'll cook you up some eggs and he says that'll be nice.

I go fetch the milk and pour some in my coffee and some over what's left of my grits, too. Velma fries up some eggs and the kitchen smells nice. This is the best breakfast in a long time.

I like Velma a bit but I s'pect I won't see her again.

Velma drives away in her pickup truck about ten-thirty. It's a green Ford — six or seven years old — a '54 I'd say. It's dented everywhere. It ain't been washed ever far as I can tell, just like Daddy's banged-up white Dodge.

Daddy says things washed just git dirty

again, and I guess they do.

I chop up the celery and onions and garlic and such for the *sauce piquante* and Daddy simmers the tomato sauce. Then we cut up the rabbits and brown 'em up in flour and oil and throw 'em in the pot. This cooks for a long time. I git my rifle and go out to the backyard at the edge of the cane field and shoot some tin cans.

We don't always have groceries but we always got lots of bullets. Daddy says it's the same thing since if you have bullets you can git groceries.

I pass the burnt-up mattress. Springs are stickin' out, like blackened brittle bones.

Daddy hollers when the *sauce piquante* is done.

He's cooked up some rice. The *sauce piquante* is real good and spicy like we like it.

Daddy takes a nap on the sofa.

I git down the money and count it.

It's thirty-five dollars, the most money I've seen so far. I put it away again.

Daddy wakes up after a while and says he's goin' back to town.

I say for what?

Business.

I say okay.

It's already too late for me to go up to school.

I say when will you be back?

He says I'm not shore, son. When I git back.

I say tonight?

He says I don't know. Depends on how the business goes.

I say okay, Daddy.

Daddy goes out and fires up the Dodge and pulls out of the driveway.

I don't s'pect to see him anytime soon.

8

Daddy ain't a bad man, least I don't think
so, though some folks might argue with
that. He says the law's just decided to git on
him and when the law decides to git on you,
it's like fleas on a hairy ole dog. You cain't
git 'em off.

The first I remember, Daddy cut a man
in a fight a coupla years after Momma
died. People who saw it said it was self-
defense, but the police dragged Daddy to
jail anyway, him bein' a LaBauve. They say
the LaBauves got Wild Injun in 'em, as I
s'pect we do. Daddy says his great-
granddaddy was a Humas Injun and they
lived wild way down in the salt marsh.
Daddy says some of 'em still do. He says
they give up speakin' Injun long ago and
started speakin' French like the Cajuns,
and then English, too. He says down there
in the salt marsh they call 'em sabines,
which Daddy says is about the same as
bein' called a nigger. He don't like that
word, same as he don't like that nigger
word.

A person who calls Daddy a sabine's gonna git a fight.

Anyway, after some lawyerin' over the man he cut, Daddy got set loose.

The second time was for illegal bull-eyein'. The game wardens had been watchin' Daddy and they caught him one night, positive he had a deer. 'Cept he didn't have no deer on him. He'd shot a bunch of coons.

The wardens wanted to know where Daddy had put the deer but Daddy stuck to his guns and said he'd just shot some coons. He had memorized the law regardin' such and it says a man can be in the woods at night with a bulleye and a single-shot rifle and a dog and be legal, long as he don't have deer or rabbits on him. Bulleyein' coons is legal. Possums, too.

He told this to the wardens, citin' chapter and verse. Daddy can be smart-alecky sometimes, I guess.

They took Daddy anyway and he spent the night in jail but the ole judge who knew Daddy let him go the next day for lack of evidence. He said them wardens were mad about that, though he was tickled.

Daddy says he felt bad about the doe he

had stashed in the palmettos before the wardens came. But he says he couldn't go back for her 'cause the wardens were watchin' him like a hawk, and it wouldn't do him no good to git caught for real, as they would make it real hard on him. Real hard.

I would've told Daddy he might consider givin' up bulleyein' deer but I knew he wouldn't listen. Daddy has particular notions, which he sticks to.

Daddy and them wardens played cat and mouse for years and they finally caught him one night — with a rabbit. Daddy was real mad that he let hisself git caught and said they would never catch him again.

That night he got liquored up and went to town and picked a fight at the police station, of all places. People said it took four or five policemen to git Daddy in the cell. He was pretty whupped when they finished with him but them policemen were pretty whupped, too.

They kept him in jail for thirty days and made him pay so much money for that rabbit that Daddy says it was the most expensive rabbit that ever walked the earth. That's when they come lookin' for me, since I was too young to be stayin' by myself, they said. Daddy says they was aimin' to put me in an orphanage but I run off when they come and hid good. He was proud of that.

Daddy never talks about Momma to me, though sometimes he looks at me in a particular way. I think he sees somethin' of Momma in me. People say I favor Momma. They say I have her eyes.

Sometimes Daddy looks at me and then he looks away from me and just shakes his head — shakes it like oh, no. Oh, no.

Sometimes when Daddy is liquored up and goes to sleep he says oh, Elizabeth. Sometimes he says Momma's name over and over and over again.

Elizabeth. Oh, Elizabeth. Please, no, Elizabeth.

9

It's late in the afternoon and the sun's cooled off so I dig me some worms in the back garden and git my cane pole and decide to go down to the Perch Hole again. I don't need fish since Daddy's left me all the *sauce piquante*.

But fishin', as Daddy says, ain't always about eatin'.

There ain't nothin' like catchin' a mess of big goggle-eye or *sac-à-lait* or havin' some greedy bass take the bait and run crazy with a hook in his mouth. Maybe even jump out of the water on you.

Daddy says bass jump like tarpons, 'cept they are a lot smaller.

I ain't never seen a tarpon or the salt water, either. Joey Hebert says his uncle caught hisself a hunderd-pound tarpon once. He says after he gits to be a lawyer and inherits his daddy's will and gits rich he's gonna buy a big boat and we'll go down to Last Island and catch us a whole mess of tarpons, and maybe some redfish, too. I've had redfish and they're the best eatin' fish there is.

I think about fishin' with Joey in his big ole boat. I guess I'll have to save up and git me a better pole by then. I guess I'd need a rod and reel.

I wander past Mandalay and there's Cassie outside with her hoe choppin' away again. That girl works hard, seems to me.

She sees me and stops choppin'.

Goin' fishin' again, Meely?

I say I am.

She says would you bring me back a mess?

I say I will, as I don't need to have 'em for supper.

She says you shore you gonna catch any?

I say I almost always catch fish though sometimes fishin' can be slow.

She says that's good 'cause I told Momma I saw you goin' fishin' yesterday and that got her in a mood for a skillet full of bream.

She says now 'course, Meely, if you don't really wanna go fishin' you could help me hoe in the garden.

I laugh and say I got my own garden to chop. Besides, like you said, white boys and colored girls cain't mix.

She laughs at this. She says you know Cancienne's corn patch?

I say I do as it's just off the bayou oppo-site the Perch Hole.

Come over there later. I'll talk to you.

Where in the corn patch?

She says anywhere. Don't worry, I'll find you.

I ax if she's serious.

She says she is.

I say okay.

She says then I'll see you there in a bit.

The fishin's pretty good. No big ones but I catch a few small bass and a whole stringer full of bream. I figger I got plenty so I head out.

I walk over by Cancienne's corn patch and think I'll never find Cassie. It must be twenty acres or more and it's hemmed in all around by cane fields. The corn's head high as it grows a lot faster than the cane does. I pick a row in the middle and duck into the patch.

I walk along for a while figgerin' I'll just come out on the other side at the haul road that leads back toward the house. I feel kinda silly draggin' all these fish along.

Pretty soon I hear a whistle. It's Cassie.

Here, Meely, she says. Right here.

I don't see her right away so I poke my head between two cornstalks and look down another row. There she is, sittin' easy in the grassy middle of the row.

I slide through, tryin' not to mash any of Mr. Cancienne's cornstalks, then lift the fish through so they don't git tangled.

Mr. Cancienne wouldn't like it. He's not an easygoin' fella.

Let's see what you've got, Cassie says.

I hold up the mess of fish.

Doggone, Meely, if you ain't some fisherman. My brother Nootsie fishes there all the time and don't git nothin' much ever.

I smile, feelin' pretty good.

Well, they're all yours, I say. I got no use for this mess.

Thanks. Momma will be pleased. Come sit.

I go and sit, pretty close.

It's my first real good look at Cassie. I like her.

She's barefooted and her feet are country feet, hard and dirty and used to walkin' over fields and gravel and such. I've got about the same feet.

She's got that same flowery dress on 'cept it's pulled up pretty much past her knees. She's got long legs and long arms and long fingers and pretty good muscles everywhere.

Her hair's in pigtails. Her face is kind of sweaty but so is mine.

I'd say she's pretty though not to her. I've never talked to girls about such.

She says it's hot ain't it, Meely?

Yeah, but not as hot as it was.

She says I got tired hoein'.

I say I don't like it, neither.

She says you grow a big garden back of that ole house?

A few long rows of this and that.

You plant it yourself?

I say I do everything. I plant it and hoe it and pick it, too.

She says what about your daddy?

I say Daddy comes and goes.

She says I don't like hoein' though I don't mind dirt so much.

Me neither, I say. It smells good, don't you think?

Smells good? Shuh, Meely, I've never heard nobody say that before.

Well, smell it next time. Not that ole black gumbo dirt that stays wet all the time. I'm talkin' about good dirt like the kind you've got in your garden.

She says well, I will. I'll smell it.

We go quiet for a while though I don't mind. It's cool here in the cornfield and peaceful too, 'cept for a car goin' by now and then on the shell road and a chirpy redwing blackbird somewhere on a stalk just gone to tassle.

Cassie says how old are you, Meely?

Fifteen. You?

Same. How come you so small?

Ain't that small, I say. Less than average is all.

Cassie gits a hoot out of this.

She says I don't mind, Meely. I think you look all right like you are.

I say I 'preciate that. I say she looks all right, too.

She says you don't favor your daddy. He's dark and got that big nose. Tall, too.

I say I take after Momma's side. Daddy's related to the Humas Injuns who live way down in the salt marsh clear to the Gulf of Mexico. They all look that way.

You got Wild Injun in you, Meely?

I s'pect I must if Daddy does.

She says huh, well ain't that somethin'.

I say how come you know so much about what Daddy looks like, Cassie?

She says like I told you, he comes round Mandalay sellin' them coons he kills. Your daddy's funny like you. He says yes sir and yes ma'am, even to colored folks. He calls Momma Miz Jackson. She gits a big kick outta that.

I say well, Daddy's different, that's for shore.

She says your daddy sells them coons for a dollar apiece though Nootsie says he could git a dollar 'n' a half.

I say I guess Daddy believes in fair as he sees fair.

Cassie draws up her knees and her dress flops down about her lap. I guess Chickie would say she's sittin' improper. It's a hard thing not to notice.

She says how is it up at your school?

I say okay. I don't always go.

Don't that git you in trouble?

Sometimes.

She says well, if we don't go that Mr. Jones gits on us. He'll whup your butt easy.

I say he sounds like Miz Breaux at Catahoula. She's itty-bitty but she can paddle.

Cassie says people say one day there will just be one school, white and colored. What you think about that, Meely?

Cassie, it don't matter to me so long as I don't have to figger algebra.

Cassie laughs. She says well, we got algebra up at Waterproof School, too.

I say your school looks okay to me. Brick and all.

She says it's okay.

I say what do they cook for dinner?

She says red beans and rice and such.

I say, huh, same as ours.

She says really? Well, do y'all git water-melon for dessert?

I say no, unfortunately.

She says we do.

I say true? I'll be dog. I wouldn't mind watermelon now and then. We git fruit cocktail from a can.

She says who's the first president of the United States?

George Washington, of course.

What about the sixteenth?

Abraham Lincoln, same as freed the slaves.

She says okay, Meely, y'all study 'bout George Washington Carver?

I say who's he?

A famous colored man.

I ain't never heard of him.

She says he invented peanut butter.

I say he did?

She says yes, he did.

I say I shore do like peanut butter.

Cassie says Meely, you shore you ain't heard of George Washington Carver? He's about as famous as colored people git.

I say no, I never did.

She says I figgered such.

I say well, 'member I don't go to school all the time.

Cassie looks at me serious. Shuh, don't

matter. I didn't figger white folks would be studyin' 'bout colored ones.

I say heck, Cassie, we don't study 'bout the Humas Injuns neither, far as I know.

She says well, that's a shame, Meely.

I say well, I s'pect it is. We've studied about some Injuns out west who whupped up on the cavalry now and then. But not one word about Daddy's Injun relations.

Cassie shakes her head disgusted. Shuh, that ain't right, Meely. Not right a'tall.

Cassie and me go quiet for a while. Then she says you like girls, Meely?

I reckon I do.

You know them girls at your school?

I don't really. My friend Joey Hebert knows 'em all.

The rich Heberts is that?

The very ones.

So you don't have a girlfriend?

I don't. But Joey's got plenty.

Cassie says well, Joey havin' plenty don't do you much good, does it?

I say no, I guess not.

Meely, you know anything 'bout girls?

I'm tempted to say I know about Mary Portier and how she don't sit proper. But as I haven't seen it myself, I don't.

I say I don't know much. Only what I've heard.

She says what's that?

How girls are different, that's all.

Cassie says what you mean?

I say different, you know.

Tell me, Meely.

I'm suddenly flustered.

Cassie laughs. She says you're blushin', Meely LaBauve!

My face is all hot and prickly so I guess I must be.

She says you ever seen what a girl has?

I say what you mean?

What a girl has? You know.

No, not exactly.

She says you want to?

I say I guess I wouldn't mind.

She says you shore?

Huh-huh.

She says if I show you what a girl has, you won't tell, will you?

I shake my head no.

She says cross your heart and hope to die? Look the devil in the eye?

I promise, Cassie.

Cassie looks about as if she's worried that somebody might be around. Then she pulls her dress up higher and is definitely sittin' improper now.

She's got on white drawers with pink and blue flowers.

She says there.

I say that looks nice.

She says I got 'em at Woolworth's in town.

I say they're real nice.

She says you wanna touch?

I say where?

She says here. She pats her Woolworths in a particular place.

I reach over. But before I git very far, Cassie takes my hand and puts it where she wants it to go, square in the middle.

It's warm there.

How's that, Meely?

I say okay.

Git a little closer, she says.

I scoot in a little closer.

Rub up and down, she says.

I do.

Cassie lays back, her head cradled in her hands.

She says keep rubbin' if you like. Think about if you was pettin' your cat.

I say I don't have no cat.

She says well then a puppy.

I say I don't have a puppy, neither, though I'd like one.

She says you know what I mean.

I say I guess I do.

Her voice gits real soft. I like the sound of it.

Soon that place is warm and her Woolworths are wet through.

She says you're a nice boy, Meely. You just go nice and slow just like you're goin'.

I say okay.

Cassie moves around a bit. Nice and slow, she says. Nice and slow.

Pretty soon Cassie takes off her Woolworths and throws 'em over her head. All of a sudden my heart goes racy and my head is full of bees.

She takes my hand again and says touch here.

I say okay.

Slow up and down, Meely.

Okay.

Pretty soon Cassie's pantin' like a dog on a blacktop road in August. She says words I don't even know.

She suddenly sits up and takes my hand in both of hers and says there, Meely, please, touch there, please. Hurry oh hurry please sweetness! Oh sweetness!

I do my best but things have gotten all wet and squirmy, like it is when you grab a slippery ole bullfrog and he's tryin' to git away.

I do my best and Cassie moans, moans loud. She says oh Jesus, sweet, sweet Jesus, oh mighty, mighty goodness!

Cassie falls back over hard, all trembly and such.

All trembly and her mouth open and her eyes closed and her face all clenched up.

Then she shivers like a chicken in the frost and goes limp.

She wilts like unwatered corn.

I jump up and look down at her. She's slumped back, drool on her chin.

I say Cassie, Cassie are you okay? Dog-gone it, Cassie, talk to me!

Things are quiet for a second and I'm 'bout half scared to death. I imagine what they'll say up at school.

First time in heaven and Meely LaBauve manages to kill somebody!

Then Cassie opens her eyes.

She smiles wide. Then laughs.

Then she says in a pretty voice come down here, precious. Come down here quick.

10

Cassie pulls me down into the grass between the corn rows. It's the first time I've held a girl so. I like the feel of her and the curves of her and the way she smells, all sweat and heaven. I like her cheek on mine and her arms around my neck.

We're a pair, for shore. Me smellin' of fish and dirty as sin. But we don't care.

Cassie says that was nice. How you feelin', Meely?

Good, I say.

You must be in a state, Cassie says.

I guess I might be.

You want your turn?

My turn?

Yeah, I've had my turn. Now it's yours, she says.

Well, okay.

She says I can tell you're in a state. I can tell by your britches.

I look down at my britches.

Oh, Lord.

She says let's see about that.

She unzips me and gets me out.

She says why Meely LaBauve, you're a skinny thang but you've got a gator in your britches!

I'm so surprised at her sayin' this that I cain't think of what to say.

She says I couldn't've imagined such.

I say I reckon I was born that way.

She hoots at this. Then she says in that soft voice, it's pretty, Meely. It's precious.

I hadn't never thought of it that way.

Real pretty, she says. Do you want me to please it?

Please it?

Please it.

I say okay.

She says okay, but just a second.

She sits up and pulls her dress clear up over her head and takes it off.

She's about like Velma, I'd say, 'cept not saggy.

She moves and then swings my legs around so they're straddlin' her legs. She spits in her hands and gets 'em all slippery and rubs the gator up and down.

I hold my breath and them bees go swarmin' in my head again.

She says we cain't do nothin' else for now.

I'm not exactly shore what else it is we could be doin'. I say that's okay, this is fine.

Meely, have you heard of rubbers?

I don't s'pose you mean boots?

She says no.

I say I have but I haven't ever seen 'em.

She says hhhm.

I say well, I hope they ain't nothin' I need right now.

She says no.

I say well, if they are I could maybe go find somebody like Joey and ax him. Or Chickie Naquin maybe, since he talks about heaven all the time.

She says heaven?

That's what Chickie calls that place.

What place?

The place I just touched.

Meely LaBauve, what a funny boy you are!

She says maybe my brother Nootsie has some rubbers but I wouldn't ax him for them.

I say no, I guess you couldn't.

Meely, do you know that some colored boys don't believe in rubbers? They'd rather be dangerous than use rubbers.

I say is that right?

She says that's right. They'll git you in trouble and then catch the first Greyhound off to New Awlins.

I say no foolin'?

She says no foolin'. And I ain't plannin' to be the kind who gits left behind.

I say that's good, Cassie.

She says well, it don't always help you git boyfriends if you feel that way.

I say I guess not.

But not every colored boy would do such a thing. Chilly wouldn't.

Who's Chilly?

She says a boy up at school.

I say a boyfriend?

She says he used to be. We broke up.

I say hhm. I'm sorry.

She says well ain't you a sweet boy, Meely.

Cassie smiles nice and then spits in her hands again and works faster.

She says how's that, Meely?

I say that's pretty good.

She says just pretty good?

I say it's real good.

Real good?

Oh goodness.

Cassie says oh goodness?

I say oh, Cassie.

She says you close?

Close to what?

Close, Meely. Close!

I say oh Lord I guess I might be.

Faster, sweetness? Slower?

I say it don't matter, Cassie. You just keep goin'.

I realize Cassie's gator's done took over my whole body.

My brain turns to worms and I git so many shivers I think I might shake apart.

Pretty soon I'm a goner.

Then I hear Cassie say oh, poor thang, Meely, you must've been savin' up for years!

I s'pect I had.

It's funny after this happens. I git real peaceful and sleepy. It's cool in the corn row and Cassie holds me close and we don't bother talkin'.

We doze off. Next I know, it's about dark and mosquitoes are eatin' us alive.

Cassie says doggone it, Meely, Momma's gonna be plenty mad if I don't git home soon! I gotta run!

She puts on her Woolworths real expert like and slips her dress back on over her head and starts to run and I say don't forgit the fish.

Oh, yeah. Cain't forgit them fish. Then Momma'll *really* be mad.

She grabs 'em up and then stops and says let's come back here tomorrow, Meely, want to?

Well, I'm goin' to school tomorrow.

Me too. After school, I mean.

Right here?

Right here, okay?

Okay.

I go home and think about eatin' and realize I'm not really hungry. I undress and flop on the bed, not botherin' to wash. I lie still, thinkin' about tomorrow and wonderin' about rubbers and such. What could be done with rubbers is prob'ly worth doin'.

Cassie's gator cain't sleep, neither. He's all hopped up again and ready to go.

We're the pair, ain't we?

I still have heaven all over my fingers and I lie with hands on my face, rememberin' what heaven smells like.

Somewhere between fish and the swamps and maybe a little watermelon. But totally different.

Totally.

Chickie Naquin's got pimples and he's fat and he don't wash and he's got no friends.

But he shore was right about heaven.

11

I git up early and go down to the bayou and take a swim. I usually swim stedda takin' baths, at least in the warm weather which is most of the time down here. The bayou's dark and cool and if it hasn't been muddied by rain for several days you can see pretty near six feet down. We've got a rickety dock which Daddy built years ago. It ain't much but it's good enough to git in and out the water without gittin' all muddy.

Back up at the house, I dry myself off with my favorite green-and-blue striped towel — one that come out of the last soap box — and put on my school clothes. I got one pair of blue jeans that's okay, no holes or rips. And a shirt Daddy brought home that he says he won in a raffle at a saloon. He calls it a golf shirt and I guess it must be 'cause there's a tiny man with a golf club sewed on it. The golfer is red, the shirt is white. It don't fit exactly but it's all right.

My boots ain't much no more and I have pretty much give up on socks since the ones I got have holes in 'em.

Daddy didn't come home last night, as I s'pected he wouldn't.

I'm too lazy to cook some grits like Velma did. So I eat what's left of the *sauce piquante* for breakfast.

It ain't bad for breakfast, really, if you add a little Tabasco. I've had gumbo for breakfast, too. Almost anything's better than no breakfast at all.

I head off up the bayou toward school. It's nearly five miles but I don't mind. Me and Daddy's alike. We can walk all day, and night, too, if we have to. Anyway, it's plenty early so I could walk slow and still git there in time.

I walk by Hog Arceneaux's place, a little shotgun shack set deep in some oaks and growed over in wisteria and honeysuckle. I pick up an oyster shell off the road just in case Pichou's in a bad mood.

Pichou's Hog's ugly ole dog and he and Hog are crazy — *couillon,* the Cajuns would say — just alike. You just never know what'll happen when you're around 'em. Sometimes Pichou'll come out and be friendly as a new pup. Sometimes he'll come out fangs bared. Worst is when he lays in the ditch in the deep Johnson grass and lets you git by, then sneaks up and takes a bite out of your hide. He got me once and once was plenty.

Since then I've crowned Pichou good with oyster shells three or four times but it don't seem to make an impression.

Pichou reminds me some of Junior in that regard. He's liable to come after me, no matter what I do.

Daddy says Pichou's a Catahoula cur dog and they're all a bit tetched. They look like they've got painted badly, bein' splotchy and spotted and about six different colors, plus they've got them different-colored eyes — usually the right one's blue and the left one's brown. It's a freakish thing to see.

Hog's house is the only one I know on this bayou that's about as run-down as our house. Hog ain't much on houses, either, I guess. Hog ain't never got married though he's an old man now. Most people avoid him 'cause he keeps hogs but don't never git rid of them. He won't even eat 'em, he just keeps 'em. They've got the run of the house. People think maybe there are unnatural things between Hog and his hogs.

Daddy and Hog are podnahs, or at least Daddy don't avoid Hog. He says I shouldn't, either, though I do sometimes. Daddy says people can be cruel and they might think they know somethin' when they don't know nothin' at all.

Everybody knows the main story about Hog. All the kids at school do. Hog, like Daddy, is a drinkin' man. Once when he was a young man and had just started to farm hogs, he got drunk. He went out to slop his hogs all liquored up and fell down and passed out for a pretty good spell.

What do hogs know?

Hog woke up a long time later and saw this big sow chewin' on his right leg. Hog pulled his leg out and his foot was pretty much missin'.

Hog crawled to the road and flagged down somebody who was happenin' by and got took to the hospital where they sewed up his stump.

When Hog got out of the hospital he wouldn't kill that sow, no way. He never killed a pig after that. He said the pig had a bit of him inside him, so why should he eat her? Wouldn't that be same as bein' a cannibal?

That sow had little pigs and they had little pigs and so on. So Hog's got all these pigs now and somehow he thinks they're all related to him.

Hog's still a drinkin' man, as far as I can tell.

It's early yet and Hog ain't out and neither is Pichou, which I'm a bit thankful for. But I know Hog's there 'cause I can hear him scratchin' on the ole fiddle he plays. It sounds sad and out of tune though I know what he's tryin' to play. It's called "Jolie Blonde." It's one of the few songs I kinda know 'cause Momma used to sing it.

Jolie blonde, 'gardez donc quoi t'as fait / tu m'as quitte' pour t'en aller.

Daddy says it's the only song Hog plays anymore and when he starts playin' it's a bit like it is when he starts talkin'. He don't know when to stop. Once he come out and played in a hurricane till the constable come out and got him and took him to shelter up at the schoolhouse. Daddy says long ago Hog played nice, and him and Momma would go and listen to Hog and some men who had a band. They'd play up at a honky-tonk way down on the water below the bayou's end — Cajun waltzes and such and everybody would dance. I can't imagine Daddy dancin' but he claims he did.

The thing about talkin' to Hog is that there's no easy way to quit, even if you don't know exactly what Hog is tryin' to tell you, which most people don't. Daddy'll go and just sit with Hog and not say nothin' much at all, which Hog don't seem to notice. Daddy'll just listen till Hog gits tired or falls asleep and then he'll leave.

I cross the shell road and am walkin' along the cane-haul road that runs for a while alongside it. A shiny red pickup pulls up. A Ford.

It's Mr. Hebert hisself.

Want a ride, Emile? he says.

It sounds funny him callin' me by my given name. I say shore.

I git in.

Francis Hebert, he says.

I know who you are. Joey's daddy.

That's right. How you doin', son?

Fine, I say. This is awful nice of you.

Were you just by Hog's place?

Walked by, yes sir. But Hog wasn't out.

Mr. Hebert shakes his head. Now that's a pitful case if there ever was one.

I say yes sir, I guess it is.

He says funny how drink ruins some people. I'll take a highball now and then, Emile, but I don't understand fallin' in the bottle.

No sir.

I guess your daddy likes a drink now and then.

Yes sir, he does.

He says well, I saw you walkin' and it's a ways up to that school and it's hot this mornin', for shore.

I say it is — *fait chaud,* as Momma used to say. I've already been swimmin'.

He says ah, your momma. Now that was a good woman. How long has it been since she passed, son?

Eight years.

Damn, that long huh?

Yes sir, that long.

Mr. Hebert says it doesn't seem like that could be right. Where does the time go, Emile?

I look at Mr. Hebert. I say well, Daddy says sometimes time don't go nowhere. Sometimes it just sits there on you like the still part of August.

Mr. Hebert swats at a deerfly that's flown in through the truck window. It buzzes and flies out fast as it flew in.

He says I hope you're not in a big hurry, Emile. I'm ridin' up the bayou slow so I can look some things over. There's a little plot of land over on this side of the bayou that ole Louby Schexnayder's tryin' to sell me. Plus I've got a whole section of cane up here that's yellowin' up bad. My foreman cain't make heads or tails out of it. But it cain't be good, whatever it is.

Hell, you lose some tonnage in a coupla hundred acres of cane and you're in serious trouble, son. But I guess you wouldn't know cane economics, now would you?

I say no sir, I wouldn't, though Daddy says a lot of cane farmers are rich 'cause the government puts 'em on the relief, same as some poor people. Anyway, I've seen some of that yellowin' cane. And no, I'm not in a rush. I started plenty early, thinkin' I'd be walkin' the whole way.

Mr. Hebert looks at me funny. He says well, your daddy don't quite have it right about cane farmers bein' on the relief. We get somethin' called price supports 'cause them Spanish people over there across the Gulf grow a lot of cane and try to sell it so cheap over here that'd we'd be driven out of business without a little help. Hell, Emile, we go out of business and this whole bayou would dry up.

I say yes sir.

He says your daddy's got lots of opinions, don't he?

I say yes sir, he does.

We come around a bend where the bayou's clearly visible. He says Emile, you swim in that ole dirty bayou?

Mr. Hebert, if I didn't swim in that

bayou I wouldn't swim nowhere.

He laughs at this then gits serious. He says I don't know if that's such a good idea, Emile. I don't think that bayou's safe. Don't you worry about gators or garfish?

Shuh, Mr. Hebert, ain't no gators where we swim. Daddy's long ago hunted them out. As for gar, they're ugly as sin but they don't bite people.

I've seen gar in that bayou long as me, son.

Oh, shore, there's big 'uns in there. Daddy caught one on a trotline that weighed two hunderd pounds. It was a lot longer'n you and me put together.

Mr. Hebert shakes his head. I gotta say, Emile, those things give me the *frissons.* Anyway, there's other things in that bayou I don't care for.

Like what?

He says once, long ago, a boy got polio swimmin' in the bayou.

What's that?

A bad disease. It cripples chirren. It can kill you.

I say well, I'll watch out for it.

Mr. Hebert shakes his head.

He don't look mean, though Joey talks like he might be sometimes. He's got a round red face and green eyes and his hair is sandy and combed back. I s'pect he uses Vitalis. Smells like it. Daddy has some at home, though he don't use it no more. On special days like Christmas I'll put a little in my hair.

Mr. Hebert don't look like he misses many meals, which I guess he wouldn't. He's dressed nice with ironed khakis and a starchy white short-sleeve shirt. I'd hate such a shirt myself. There's two fat cigars in the shirt pocket. The truck smells a little like cigars after they've been smoked.

He says does Joey go swimmin' with you sometime?

He's been once or twice to Poule D'eau Curve.

Emile, I don't like that.

I say well, I don't know about polio but otherwise it's not dangerous. Lots of boys on the bayou go swimmin' down there. Joey's a good swimmer.

He says Emile, I don't want you to take this the wrong way but I wish you'd stay away from Joey.

I look at Mr. Hebert. Maybe he is mean after all.

Well, Joey's my only friend, really. I kinda know Chickie Naquin but folks say Chickie ain't got no friends so I guess he cain't be one. Anyway, it ain't the same as knowin' Joey.

He says well, Emile, Joey's got a real future ahead of him and everything I've got's gonna be his one day. I don't want anything bad happenin' to him.

You mean like polio?

Yes, things like that.

I say heck, I know all about Joey's future and how he's gonna go to Tulane and be a lawyer and such. I'm pretty well excited about that myself, as Joey will buy a boat and we'll git to go fishin'. Anyways, Joey and me look out for each other.

He says Joey told you about that?

I say about bein' a lawyer or goin' fishin?

About law school.

He did. He says he's gotta be a lawyer or else you'll cut him out of your will.

Mr. Hebert shakes his head again. He told you *that*, too?

I say yes sir, he did.

Mr. Hebert looks at me real close. He says well, I guess Joey tells you pretty near everything, don't he?

I say I guess he does.

Mr. Hebert just nods. Then he takes one of them cigars out of his shirt pocket and puts it in his mouth. He chews on it a bit but he don't light it. We're only drivin' about twenty-five miles an hour, but Mr.

Hebert slows down even more, then stops.

He points over beyond my side of the truck. He says that's it, Louby's little spread. Nice, huh? He's got two hundred acres of real good land, Emile. I've offered him a hundred thousand.

Is that dollars, Mr. Hebert?

It is, Emile. Cash. I know it sounds like a lot but, hell, for soil like he's got, it's worth it. I'll even let him keep the house and two acres around it.

Mr. Hebert laughs. He says as you know, Emile, I already got a house.

I think about the thirty-five dollars that Velma give me and how much it is compared to a hunderd thousand. I cain't start to figger the difference.

I say Mr. Hebert, can I ax you somethin'?

What's that?

Is it actually true you got all the money in the world?

Mr. Hebert chomps on that cigar so hard that he about chomps it in two. He takes it out of his mouth and spits tobacco out the window. He pulls a bit of tobacco off his lower lip.

He looks at me daft like. I almost think he might smile but he don't.

He says Joey didn't say *that*, did he?

Well, he did but he's not the only one. All the kids at school say that. Teachers too.

Mr. Hebert looks at me serious. He says no I don't have all the money in the world. People exaggerate. Even the Rockefellers don't have all the money in the world, though they've got a lot of it.

I say who's that?

He says they're some rich family up north someplace.

I say well, you've got the most money on this bayou, I bet.

He says Emile, I wouldn't say if I did. It's not polite to talk about those things. And money comes with a lot of responsibility, too. Us Heberts have always worked hard and taken our responsibilities serious.

I think about this a second, then say well, Joey says you don't do no real work no more. He says you just drive round on your tractor mower and drive round in your truck lookin' at your land and c'leckin' the money off it.

Mr. Herbert puts the truck in gear and we start movin' again. He looks at his cigar, which is about chewed in half, then throws it out the window.

Well, lemme tell you, Emile, I wish it was that simple. But there's lots to be done to keep a cane farm runnin' proper. Paper-work, taxes, God knows what else. You wouldn't believe how much money I have to give to the government every year. A good cane farmer works mostly with his head not his back and head work can be hard, too.

I say like algebra you mean?

He says algebra?

Yes sir, algebra. That's about the hardest thing I can think of to do with your head even though I haven't done it yet.

Ah, I see.

I say you got any ghosts in that big house of yours?

He says Emile, as a good Catholic man I'm tellin' you there's no such thing. That's superstitious nonsense.

I believe that, Mr. Hebert. I myself ain't superstitious, neither.

Then why'd you ask?

Joey once told such to Junior Guidry and his bunch.

Did he?

I say yes sir, he did and I got a big kick out of that. He had Junior goin' for a while. Joey's smart and can talk circles around Junior, which I like to see. Junior didn't know what to make of it. I give Junior the Evil Eye once and he didn't know what to make of that, neither.

Evil Eye?

Yes sir. Just somethin' Daddy showed me. A trick. You wanna see it?

Mr. Hebert looks at me careful. He says I don't think I do, Emile. I think I'll take your word for it.

He goes quiet for a moment, then says Joey's not in trouble with that Junior Guidry is he? That boy's rough.

I say he shore is rough, Mr. Hebert. Heck, nearly everybody who's not in Junior's bunch is in trouble with Junior.

He says well, that whole family is rough. They've got eight kids and the daddy drinks and pretty much beats 'em all when he's drunk, the momma too, I hear. Junior's older brother got killed drivin' drunk five years ago. That boy was only seventeen.

Yes sir, I knew that.

Strangest damn thing I ever heard of.

The wreck?

No, Emile, that boy — Bo was his name — had gotten in a bad way with one of them Ardoin girls way up the bayou. You know them Ardoins? Not a bad family, really. They've got a nice little cane farm and some winter cabbage. They do all right. 'Cept the daddy, Cleo, couldn't manage to have nothin' but girls. But, shuh, God gives what God gives, I guess.

I say yes sir. I know of 'em. There's a couple of Ardoins at school.

He says anyway, Bo just before he got killed had gotten one of those older Ardoin girls in trouble, if you know what I mean, and Cleo was hot under the collar, lemme tell you, Guidry meanness or not. So he was after Bo to marry her, even if he had to git out his shotgun. Then Bo gits his fool self killed before this can be arranged.

Mr. Hebert stops a second to spit out the window.

Then he says now I always thought of Cleo as a man with sense but he's a religious man, as most of us are out here, thank God, and he just cain't stand the idea he's gonna have a bastard in his family. So he goes and gits the ole retired priest, Father Eschete, out of his house way over on Bayou Moustique and drives him over to the funeral home where they've taken Bo. On the way there, he picks up his daughter who's in a bad way and when they git there the ole priest marries her to the corpse.

Mr. Hebert stops for a moment and gits the second cigar out of his shirt pocket, fiddles with it a bit, then sticks it in his mouth.

He says imagine, Emile, marryin' that poor girl to a dead man. Now, I know this is true because I'm good personal friends with Tub Falgout the undertaker and he saw it himself.

He searches his shirt pocket for a match, finds a box of them, and lights his cigar. He lets the smoke out real slow. It rises in a little cloud before bein' sucked out the window.

He says now you cain't blame Cleo for not wantin' a bastard in his family 'cause no man does, Emile, but isn't that the craziest thing you ever heard, son?

I think about this real hard. I have admit it might be the craziest thing I've heard yet, outside of Hog's eat-up foot. But it makes me think there's just lots of crazy things that are bound to happen in the world.

I say it is peculiar, Mr. Hebert. That's for shore.

Mr. Hebert don't have no more to say and we make one more stop, at a field where about a quarter of the cane seems to have turned yellow as Mr. Hebert said it had. He grunts and nods and says damn all, though not really to me. And I cain't think of anything else I wanna ax him. We're pretty close to school anyway. He drives on and up into the circular driveway at school and lets me out.

Thanks I say.

He looks at me, shakin' his head.

He just says be careful, Emile. Be careful. And watch that Guidry boy.

I say I will.

He don't say anything more about me stayin' away from Joey, which I'm glad he don't.

Even though Mr. Hebert has drove slow, I've got here plenty early. I go up and sit in the cool of the bleachers 'neath an oak next to the softball field.

I try to think about ball but think some about this poor girl who married a dead man. I think about Momma.

I decide I shouldn't be thinkin' about either of those things, so I think about Cassie instead.

12

Junior Guidry and his bunch come early to school, bats and gloves slung over their shoulders.

I wish I wasn't so high up on the bleachers, all visible. Junior sees me right away.

If it ain't the runt, he says. They let you outta jail for school? Your daddy in prison yet?

I ignore him like Miz Lirette says I should.

He says you plannin' to lose at softball, Mealy Mouth?

I keep ignorin' him.

He says I don't know why trash like the LaBauves bother with school. They don't know shit from Shinola and never will.

I'm about at the end of ignorin' Junior.

He says to his bunch y'all know about sabines? Mealy Mouth tries to pass hisself off as white but he's really a damn sabine.

I stand up.

Junior says what, you want a piece of me, Mealy Mouth? Shuh! I've wiped my ass with things bigger'n you!

Junior thinks this is clever and he hawhaws real loud. His gang starts hawhawin', too. Like jackasses, if you ax me.

I decide I do want a piece of Junior though I s'pect I'll git whupped. I take a step down the bleachers.

Luckily, Miz Lirette drives up in her Ford Galaxy 500. She's what they call the duty teacher and has come early to see things over.

She pulls her car up in the parkin' spot not too far from the softball field. She don't see me but she comes over to see what's goin' on.

Hello, Junior, she says.

He says in his polite voice hello, Miz Lirette.

This about makes me snort. I imagine Junior is what Daddy would call a hypocrite.

Miz Lirette spies me up in the bleachers. Hello, Emile. I'm glad you're here.

Hello, Miz Lirette, I say.

I'm tempted to say that until Junior showed up I was glad I was here, too. But I don't.

Other boys come soon enough, includin' Joey dropped off by his momma. Joey says hi, Meely, and tosses me his extra glove.

He says I heard you and Daddy had a little talk.

I say we did.

He says Daddy says you're a character, too.

I'm not shore exactly how to take this.

We divide up the teams as usual. The galoots against us.

There's a big crowd around now so I walk past Junior and as I go I give him half an Evil Eye.

I just turn one of my eyeballs backward like Daddy showed me and keep the other square on Junior.

As I do this I say *gris-gris* on you, Junior Guidry. You're ugly as a possum's ass. The sabine devil's gonna git in your head. You're gonna strike out and everybody's gonna laugh at you.

Daddy wouldn't like me sayin' possum's ass. He don't cuss and don't believe I should, either.

Junior wants to go for me but the eye's got him stopped. He's stuck in his tracks for a second and I slide past, headin' for shortstop.

Junior wants to play worse than he wants to mash me up.

The galoots come to bat first. They always do.

Roddy Bergeron, who's practically Junior's slave, is lead off. Joey says Roddy don't fart 'less Junior says he's allowed. He a pretty good hitter, though. He clobbers one to center field where Joey plays. Joey's only thirteen, younger than most of us, but he's fast. He catches it.

Then comes Jerome Giroir. He's about as fat as Chickie Naquin 'cept he don't have pimples and he wears better clothes. His daddy's got cane land too, which prob'ly impresses Junior.

He clobbers another one to center field. Joey runs hard and catches that one, too. Jerome moans like a constipated cow.

Po-Boy Trahan is s'posed to bat next but I see Junior talkin' to him. Junior usually bats cleanup but he's mad and wants to bat now and what Junior wants he usually gits. He's got a big black bat he's bought at a fancy sportin' goods store in town. Once when he wasn't lookin' I picked it up. It's heavy as a six-foot gator to me.

Junior glares at me over at shortstop.

I glare back.

T-Boy Orgeron, our pitcher, lays a fat one right over the middle of the plate.

Junior swings mighty and hits a long ball clear over the fence in left field.

Far foul, thank God.

T-Boy pitches again, this one with a little more arc and spin.

Junior swings so hard that I can hear the wind from his bat clear to shortstop. He pops up a foul way behind the backstop clear to the shell road. We wait while somebody fetches the ball. We're lucky it didn't sail all the way into the bayou.

I tell Johnny Lirette on third and Billy Cancienne on second to start sayin' strike out, Junior. They look at me like I'm crazy. Junior's like Babe Ruth and Mickey Mantle both. He never strikes out. Not too many people do in softball.

But they start chantin' it anyways. Strike out, Junior, strike out.

I say it too. By the time the ball is throwed back the outfield is chantin' too.

Junior spits in his hands and rubs up and down the bat and says morons real loud. I'm gonna show you sorry bastids.

I go over and have a word with T-Boy. Big arc, I say. Junior don't like them big arcs.

T-Boy's a good pitcher. He lays one out there that floats at Junior like a fat pigeon in slow motion.

Junior swings so hard he just about falls down.

He misses clean.

107

The air's pretty near still for a moment. The galoots is out.

Then Junior comes chargin' after me with that big black bat of his.

I look around fast. Miz Lirette ain't here no more. She's prob'ly gone into school.

I let Junior get about three quarters way to shortstop. He's got that bat cocked back about to throw it.

He does and it comes whirrin' like a helicopter knee high. I jump up and it whirs right under me.

Junior's yellin' like a maniac. When he's about four foot away, I juke left and run right.

I juke ole Junior right out of his shoes.

He slips down hard on the infield dirt. I hear him cuss but he gits up fast.

I'm already haulin' ass for the school-house.

Junior's right behind. He won't catch me in a footrace, no way, but I don't wanna git cornered.

I go scootin' up the schoolhouse steps and look back. Junior's snortin' like that mean red bull in Eustus Daigle's pasture.

I got no choice. I run through the door and go flyin' down the hall.

Miz Breaux steps out of a classroom and snatches at me as I go by.

She misses.

Then she sees why I'm runnin'.

She steps out in front of Junior. She says stop, Junior, but he plows right into her.

She goes flyin' down the hall like a rag doll. Junior falls too, flat on his face. He skids like he's goin' into second base on his belly.

Miz Lirette steps out of her classroom.

Junior Guidry, she yells real loud. Are you crazy?!

Funny, but itty-bitty Miz Breaux ain't knocked out. She gits up before Junior does.

She brushes herself off and walks over to Junior, who's barely made it to his knees.

She grabs him hard by the ear and pulls him up to his feet.

She looks down the hall at me and says Emile, into my office. Right now. Both of you.

I go on my own. Junior gits pulled in by his ear. He's already sayin' it hurts, Miz Breaux. It hurts.

He's limpin' I'm happy to see. Grabbin' at his left knee.

She axes what's this about?

Meely cussed me, Junior says. He looked at me funny.

Miz Breaux looks at me.

I say well, I might've called him a possum name but only after he called me a sabine and more. Then he struck out and threw a bat at me and come after me. That's why I was runnin'. Go ax Joey Hebert. Go ax anybody.

Liar! says Junior. Goddam liar!

Miz Breaux yanks hard on Junior's ear. She says real loud Junior Guidry, nobody talks like that in my office! Do you understand me?

She says this so loud that even Junior is surprised.

Miz Lirette has come in. Miz Breaux tells her go git me Joey.

This is good for me, as everybody likes Joey.

Joey comes and tells what he knows. He says he don't know who cussed who and who looked at who crossways but he does know that Junior struck out and come after me. He says Meely didn't try to fight back. He ducked the bat then run for his life.

Miz Breaux looks at Junior. She looks at me. She tells me to go to class and she'll deal with me later. She tells Joey thank you.

She says to Junior you're a disgrace, Junior Guidry. Nobody throws bats at people at my school. Somebody could have been killed.

Junior glares at me and glares at Joey. He mighta glared at Miz Breaux but he's scared of her, I can tell.

Me and Joey go out and we hear Miz Breaux tellin' Junior to bend over.

There's about ten or eleven loud whacks.

I'm hopin' Junior's cryin' but I s'pect he ain't.

Junior whines but he prob'ly ain't the cryin' kind.

The day goes by fidgety.

In the cafeteria at dinner Chickie says he saw Junior's daddy come to git him. He's heard Junior's been expelled for a week.

Miz Breaux calls me in in the afternoon and says Emile, I'm not gonna punish you this time, though I don't like people carryin' on in my halls that way. But you had a good excuse to run and I'm pleased you ran instead of fought. Please tell me if Junior bothers you. I won't tolerate it.

I say thank you, Miz Breaux.

I don't tell her Junior bothers me all the time. Daddy says people should try to handle their own troubles.

I go back to Miz Lirette's class where there's a history lesson. It's that story again about the Injuns and somebody named Crazy Horse who tussled with Custer out west. He whupped Custer good and died proud though the Injuns somehow ended up on the short end of the stick. That figgers.

It's funny to think about Crazy Horse and the Humas Injuns down in the salt marsh and how I've got Wild Injun in me and how we've all come to be called sabines by people like Junior.

I wonder if there was cowboys down in the salt marsh back then and whether my great-great-granddaddy mighta whupped them too.

It's all curious.

One thing about a fidgety day is I don't think too much about heaven or Cassie.

I also forgit to ax Chickie or Joey about rubbers.

13

I walk all the way home and go in and check to see if maybe Daddy has showed up. He hasn't.

In the kitchen, I fix a sandwich with white bread Daddy brought home. White bread and brown sugar. I like the bread 'cause it's got the Lone Ranger on the wrapper. I seen him once at the movies.

I wash my sandwich down with cistern water and head up past Mandalay toward the Perch Hole.

I wonder if Cassie will really be there. On the long walk home I've managed to git my mind back on heaven.

Cassie's gator is thinkin' about heaven, too.

I cross over the gravel road from the bayou-side and start to cut across the grass patch that leads to Cancienne's cornfield.

Junior Guidry walks out of the corn patch. Roddy Bergeron and Jerome Giroir, too.

There's about six of 'em.

Well, Mealy Mouth, you happy with

what you did to me?

I figger he don't really want an answer so I don't give one.

He says I'm gonna teach you a lesson, sabine.

I try to figger my chances. I can prob'ly outrun most of 'em a short ways but there's Po-Boy Trahan with them. He's rabbit fast.

I might make it back to the bayou and try to outswim 'em. But if they catch me they'll drown me for shore.

I wonder if Cassie's around.

I think about the Evil Eye.

I see Junior's got a nice big stick with him.

He says don't go tryin' none of that voodoo shit on me this time, Mealy Mouth, it ain't gonna work.

I decide quick. I say the *gris-gris* was give to me by my Injun grandma and it's powerful wicked. If you lay a finger on me, I'll turn your guts to worms. Besides, my daddy's out there in the field with his twelve-gauge double-barrel and he's Wild Injun mad. I've told him you called me a sabine and he wants to blow your head off. I prob'ly cain't stop him now unless I say you've turned nice. Lemme be, Junior. Or else.

Junior practically snarls at me.

Liar, Mealy Mouth! Lyin' sabine bastid! My uncle's with the police in town and they throwed your daddy in the drunk tank last night. I'll bet he's still sleepin' it off.

He says liar liar liar! Hah, sabine liar!

He haw-haws again.

This does stump me for a second.

Doggone it, Daddy.

Sometimes I could just strangle Daddy.

I look at Junior and give him half an Evil Eye. I raise my hands above my head and say the *gris-gris* spirits have told me that Daddy has broke outta jail and has killed two police officers already, 'cludin' your uncle. It's already been on the radio. You better lemme go, Junior, or you're next.

Bullshit, he says. I've got your runty little ass this time.

I'm about to lay the full Evil Eye on him when Junior says y'all don't look directly at him. Look at his knees. Tackle him down and we'll throw this sack over his head. Then we'll kick his sorry ass, good.

I notice that Roddy Bergeron's got a pretty good sack.

I say to myself well dang, Meely, you're in for it now. I wonder what Daddy would do.

Heck, I know what Daddy would do.

I say Junior how'd you git to be as ugly as you've got? Do you practice a lot? How come you still wet the bed?

Junior comes a runnin' hard.

I juke him out again and I kick him as he slides by. It ain't a solid kick, unfortunately.

He cusses loud and grabs at me and yells y'all git him!

I run hard but trip and Po-Boy Trahan's on me like mange. He's not much bigger than me and I roll him off and scratch for his eyes.

I git him good in the face and he wails but next thing I know Roddy Bergeron's got that sack and he's tryin' to put it on my head.

I swing blind and catch somebody's head, maybe Roddy's. He cusses too and then they just all pile on.

I feel Junior's stick across my back and it knocks the wind out of me. The sack goes over my head and somebody's got my arms pinned. I kick at shins and connect pretty good and somebody hollers.

Then there's a fist on the side of my head and then the other and that stick again and then a kick in the ribs.

Then somebody socks me square in the mouth and I taste blood.

I'm down on the ground by this time and I try to curl up in a ball best as I can but it's hard.

That's when I hear Cassie's voice.

Stop it, she yells. Stop it now!

The whole world stops for a second.

Junior says who the hell are you?

And then there's another voice that says who the hell are *you?*

It's an awful big voice.

People have let me go and I pull off the sack and look up. I notice my hands are shakin'.

There's Cassie at the edge of the cornfield with the biggest colored boy I've ever seen. He's a giant.

He makes that galoot Junior look little.

The giant speaks up. Git away from that boy.

I notice legs startin' to move away from me. Not Junior's though.

Then Junior says nigger, stay out of this.

Then the giant says Cassie, did you hear what he said? That sissy-assed white boy over there just called me a nigger. Can you imagine?

He says come over here, white boy, so I can spank you.

Junior don't move.

The giant says goddam you, white boy, I

said git your sissy ass over here now!

He screams this and then he charges.

Doggone it if he ain't quicker than a greased mink.

He's got Junior by the collar of his shirt before Junior can move an inch.

He lifts big ole Junior up like some rag doll and holds him there for a second.

I notice that Junior's peed his pants.

The giant says, Junior — is that your name, Junior? — well, Junior, I'm gonna let you go. Then you're gonna bend over.

I look around. Roddy and that bunch's eyes are poppin' out of their heads.

They're like rabbits at the side of the road with a dog on their ass, ready to bolt.

The giant pushes Junior down rough.

Bend over he says. Goddam bend over or I'm gonna kick your sorry white ass all the way down to the tip of Catahoula Bayou.

Junior picks hisself up and bends over.

The giant looks at me. He starts to unbuckle his belt and there's a gasp from the galoots. But then he stops and picks up the big stick Junior was holdin' and holds it up toward the sky as though examinin' it.

He says yeah, this will do. Now, Meely, you wanna do it?

I have no idea how he knows my name.

I'm woozy but I say shore I do.

I git Junior's stick and I realize I do have Wild Injun in me. I give him a good crack across his butt. He yowls.

I give him another, then another.

I say one more for good measure. I give him a harder one and he yowls again.

I look at the giant and say can I whack the rest of them boys, too?

He says shore, why not? Which one of 'em you want first?

The whole bunch takes off, like ducks flushed from a pond, 'cept Junior, who's stuck, in his peed pants, like a possum in a spotlight.

The giant says you done with this one?

Yeah.

You lettin' him off easy. If I were you I'd give him a coupla more. Upside the head.

I say I've give him enough for now.

He says well, Junior, whatever your name is I guess you can go. Just don't lemme catch you round this cornfield no more, you hear me? You leave my podnah Meely alone. You got that?

Junior nods.

The giant says that ain't good enough. I want to hear you. You got that, Junior?

Junior looks down at the ground. He says I got it.

I s'pect he don't mean it.

The giant says well git the hell outta here 'fore we decide you ain't had enough.

Junior finds his legs and backs off slow like the giant might jump him again. Then he turns and runs off, but it's plain he's hurtin'.

I am, too.

14

Cassie says Meely, you're busted up perty good.

I say that I am.

She says you better lemme see after that.

I'll be okay.

You got blood on your chin.

I wipe it off on my sleeve. I feel bad 'cause it's my golf shirt Daddy give me. Blood don't wash out very easy, not even with store-bought soap. I know 'cause I do the washin' at my house.

Cassie says this is Chilly from up at school. He's my ex-boyfriend. The one I tole you about.

Chilly laughs hard. He says how ya doin', Meely?

Then he looks at Cassie. He says Cassie, I cain't believe you're still mad at me. Redonna Mouton is just my friend. I come all the way down here to find you to explain.

Cassie says your friend my butt, Chilly Cox. Loretta told me everything you did up at the school fair with Redonna. Loretta

121

told me you had a pint of liquor and y'all went over into the cane field. Plenty people saw you go.

I don't s'pose colored people can blush, really. But Chilly looks like he wants to.

He says Cassie, Cassie, Cassie, girl, ain't nothin' happened out there. We just had us a few pops of whiskey's all. We just talked.

Cassie says my foot. Talked about what? Everybody knows about Redonna Mouton. That girl cain't keep her drawers on. You cain't neither, Chilly Cox.

I'm a little surprised Cassie is sayin' this knowin' what it is I know.

Chilly shakes his head exaggerated like.

He says, how come it is that Loretta's always in my bizness, anyways?

Cassie says Chilly, you colored boys don't understand but us colored girls gotta stick together 'ginst y'all.

Chilly busts out laughin' at this.

Cassie shakes her head and looks real stern though I can tell she's not really. She says we'll see about that, Chilly Cox. Right now we gotta look after Meely.

I say it's okay, Cassie. I'll just go home and clean up.

No, Meely. You need some tendin'. Your daddy back yet?

No.

She says well then you come over and let Momma look at you.

It's hot and I do feel a little woozy still. My mouth hurts and my back does too. Come to think of it, I hurt all over.

I say thanks much, Chilly. You shore put the fear of God into Junior and his gang.

He says they look like a bunch of bullies.

I say that they are.

What's that Junior got against you, Meely?

I say if I knew that, Chilly, I'd be that Einstein fella. Junior's been on my back about since I've had a back.

Chilly says well, I hope you don't mind me tellin' Junior we're podnahs. I figger if he thinks that, he might leave you alone.

I say Chilly, after what you done, we *are* podnahs.

Chilly laughs.

Cassie says Meely's daddy's the gator man of this here bayou and he do what he pleases, don't ax nobody for nothin'. He's got more truck with the colored then he do the whites. This sits the wrong way with some folks.

I hadn't really thought about it that way.

Cassie says plus Meely's got the Wild Injun in him from his daddy's side. I guess some people round here ain't got no more use for Injuns than they have for us coloreds. Far as they're concerned, we're all just niggers together.

Chilly shakes his head. He says well, ain't that somethin'. I ain't never met me no Injun before.

Well, Chilly, I'm awful glad to meet you as Junior and his bunch were turnin' me into a punchin' bag.

Chilly laughs big as an oak. He says well, Meely, you ain't big enough to make a decent sack of corn but you give 'em hell, I'll say that.

Cassie says were you scared, Meely?

I say well, I was gittin' a little worried when they got that sack over my head. If I hadn't tripped I mighta got away 'cept for that Po-Boy Trahan. He's the only boy in school who can outrun me.

Cassie says well, c'mon, Meely, let's go to Momma's.

I've seen Miz Jackson out in her yard many times. I've always waved and she does, too, but I cain't remember talkin' to her. Sometimes I just feel solitary and got no use for talkin'.

I decide I wouldn't mind a little lookin' after.

We walk about a half mile to Cassie's house, usin' the Grassy Road stedda the shell one. Chilly says we done whupped

Junior and his whole cavalry but you never know about people like that. They could come back with guns and such.

I hadn't thought about that. The cavalry part, either. I think about that Crazy Horse fella and how he whupped the cavalry good but lost out anyways.

Miz Jackson is sittin' on the porch rockin'. She sees us all comin' and I guess she don't know what to make of it as she puts her hand up over her eyes like she's lookin' into the sun. We git close enough for her to see us and she says Lord, girl, what's goin' on here?

Cassie says hi, Momma, this here is Meely and he's been hurt.

She says I know who Meely is and I can see that he has. C'mon in the house, chile, and let's look at you.

She looks at Chilly and says Chilly, I see you found her after all.

Yes ma'am, I did.

Miz Jackson's about as old as Daddy far as I can tell. She's rail thin like Cassie and stands straight. She's got on a dress that I figger's been made from corn sacks. I know 'cause it's brown with big blue flowers on it just like the ones we buy our seed corn in. She's got a blue kerchief tied round her head.

Cassie's house is a little white house made just like all the other little white houses the colored folk who work in sugar live in. We walk through the parlor into the kitchen where Miz Jackson pulls a chain on a light hangin' from the ceilin'. The light comes on though it's not very bright.

The kitchen is neat as a deer track. Somethin's cookin' on the stove and it smells good.

She says Meely, lemme look at you.

Cassie says Momma did some nursin' long ago.

I stand still and she goes over me. I can already feel my top lip's all swelled up. There's a knot on my head. She presses here and there and axes does this or that hurt. She says hhm and huh-huh now and then.

She says you'll likely have a bit of a shiner. She says open your mouth. I do.

She says does this tooth hurt? She grabs an upper between two fingers and jiggles. It don't hurt, really.

She says it don't seem to be loose.

She says let's have this bloody shirt off. I take it off and she says my, we better put somethin' on the welts back here. Cassie, go into the bathroom and git me a wet wash-cloth and some of that drugstore salve.

She says who beat you like this, Meely?

Junior Guidry and his bunch. Lucky Cassie and Chilly come along otherwise they'd still prob'ly be beatin' me.

Chilly says Meely give 'em heck, Miz Jackson, but he was outnumbered six to one.

She shakes her head, disgusted. She says I know them Guidrys. They ain't one of 'em got the sense they was born with. Meely, I just don't understand that kind of meanness.

She says Chilly, I s'pose you weighed in?

Yes ma'am. Cassie yelled for me and I couldn't just stand there.

Well, you done right but you watch out, you hear? I wouldn't put nothin' past them Guidrys.

Chilly says yes ma'am, I will.

Cassie comes back with the washcloth and the salve. Miz Jackson pats the cloth gentle on my back then rubs the salve on all soft like. She says you better not put that bloody shirt back on. I'll give you an ole T-shirt of Cassie's.

I say thank you.

She says how's your daddy keepin', Meely?

I still don't know what to make of Junior's story about Daddy bein' in the drunk tank.

I just say he's fine, Miz Jackson. He's off in town on business.

She says well, it was awful nice of you to give us that mess of fish the other day. Since Mister died things git tight in this ole house sometimes.

Yes ma'am, I know how that is.

I know you do, Meely. Did you know that long ago your momma used to come by some?

She did?

She shore did. She sat right here at this kitchen table and we'd talk woman talk. She was a sweet woman. A sense of humor, too.

When Miz Jackson says this she grins and I see she's got them same strong white teeth as Cassie. 'Cept one of them's all gold and such. It looks nice.

It's throwed me a bit that Momma's been here in this house.

Miz Jackson says you favor your momma.

I say people tell me that.

She says your momma always said you were a sweet boy. I bet you miss her.

I say yes ma'am, I do.

She says your momma always said your daddy was a handful. She said that's why a woman has to have big hands!

Miz Jackson laughs deep when she says that then she goes quiet. She says my mister was a bit of a handful, too. But the only really bad thing he ever done was die.

I don't quite know what to say about that. I think about her and Momma sittin' at the table here just yakkin' away.

Miz Jackson says once when you weren't more than a bitty baby your momma brought you over here and you and Cassie crawled round together. You were a pair, for shore, wrasslin' around on the floor together.

I look at Cassie, who's got a grin on her face. I had no idea I'd knowed Cassie for so long. I shore didn't know that we'd crawled around on the floor.

I wonder if this explains why we've got to be friends and such so quick.

When I think about yesterday, I suddenly git all shivery.

I wonder if Miz Jackson would be tendin' me so if she knew what Cassie and I did. A momma prob'ly wouldn't think it was nice. I doubt my momma would've.

Miz Jackson notices my shivers and says look at this poor chile, he's got a chill. Cassie, run go fetch that shirt for Meely.

Cassie goes into a little room off the kitchen and comes back with a white

T-shirt. It's torn a bit in the sleeve but clean and soft. I put it on and it smells some like Cassie, which I don't mind.

Miz Jackson says you wanna lie down a bit, Meely?

I say no ma'am. I s'pose I better git home.

She says there's no need to rush. You can spend the night here if you want to. We've got a sofa in the parlor. It don't look like much but it's comfortable.

I think about this. Then I say well, maybe Daddy will be home and he might be worried if I'm not there.

She says well, supper's 'bout ready. You might as well stay for that.

I say I couldn't really.

She says I'm cookin' turnips and coon stew. My boy Nootsie run over a coon crossin' the road this mornin' and skinned it for me. Usually I barbecue 'em but I was too lazy to go out and make a fire.

My mouth's all sore but my stomach's all growly. I don't know why but I feel bashful at times like this.

Cassie says c'mon, Meely, have some supper with us. Now Chilly here, we won't be able to run off with a stick.

Chilly chuckles. He says thanks for axin' me to stay, Cassie. I think I will.

I say well, I will too, thank you.

The coon is good, tender and such, and the gravy is delicious over rice. I eat and eat and eat till I'm stuffed.

15

It's dark and lonesome when I git home, carryin' my golf shirt in a paper sack Miz Jackson give me. Daddy's not come home. Maybe Junior's right. He's prob'ly in jail.

My back's hurtin' pretty much where Junior whacked me. My neck's stiff.

I find a candle and light it and carry it to the bathroom where I peer in the mirror. I'm pretty much a mess. I've got a fat lip and a pretty good shiner comin' on.

I splash a little water on my face and brush my teeth and when I spit there's still a little blood. I rinse out my mouth good and spit again. I pee and go to my bedroom.

I shuck my jeans and lie there on my stomach in my drawers and Cassie's T-shirt. It's comfortin' that it smells like her. But I'm too beat to think about heaven.

I go to sleep and dream and wake and dream and wake again.

I dream of Momma, the same dream I always have.

We're sittin' in the livin' room all of us, Momma, Daddy, the baby, and me.

The baby's just a baby but she walks and talks and giggles and such. She sits on my lap and we sing a song in Cajun, one Momma taught us.

Fais dodo it goes, a lullaby. When we finish everybody laughs and claps, Daddy 'specially.

That's all there is to that dream, over and over again.

I never seen the baby so I have no idea what it looked like. But in my dream she's got black hair and brown eyes and pale white skin like Momma. Her dream name is Katy though I'm not shore she ever got named. It don't say on Momma's tomb and for some reason it don't seem a right question to ax Daddy.

I remember enough to know that Momma was happy that she was havin' the baby. Daddy, too, as I recall.

I don't know what went wrong. I know the woman that was tendin' Momma got all worried and sent for the doctor in town. But it took a long time over these bad roads and by the time he got out here it was too late.

I remember bein' told to go out in the yard and wait. I remember comin' in from the backyard catchin' mosquito hawks off the clothesline and seein' the doctor tall with his hand on Daddy's shoulder.

Daddy was cryin'. First time I'd ever seen Daddy cry.

I remember he looked up at me and said your momma's gone, son.

I said gone where, Daddy?

She's died, son. Momma's died. Our little baby, too.

I said no, Daddy, no.

He said yes it's true, son.

I said please, Daddy, no.

He just shook his head. I remember his eyes was all watery and red.

I remember takin' off runnin' I didn't care where. Little as I was, I ran and ran and ran till the next thing I know I was at the woods and I just kept goin' even then. I thought if I stopped runnin' I would bust open and everything would spill out. I ran till I fell and got up and ran some more and soon it was dark and I fell again and was too tired to move. Things crept and moaned and crawled about in the woods around me but I didn't care. Mosquitoes ate me up but I could barely move to swat 'em.

Daddy says the doctor told him he oughta call the police to go find me but

Daddy says he knew nobody could find me but him. He come trackin' me in the mornin'. He says if I'da run much more I'da run plumb outta the Catahoula Swamp. He says it was an impressive piece of runnin', which I guess it was.

They buried Momma and the baby in the same coffin. I hadn't cried none in the woods but at the funeral somethin' give way and I cried and cried and cried. It all come out at once and I couldn't no more stop it than a man can stop the rain fallin'.

Daddy didn't cry at all. He just stood there silent lookin' out toward nowhere. I guess he give up on cryin' then.

I think it was the start of Daddy givin' up on things.

For a long time afterward I would wake up and think Momma was in the kitchen fixin' coffee or makin' gumbo or such. I would wake up and think she had her hand on my forehead sayin' wake up, Meely, cher, *réveiller, cher 'tit chou.* But she wouldn't be there.

I quit thinkin' that after a while and now about all that's left of Momma is this dream and a pitcher that Daddy give me. I keep it on my dresser.

In that pitcher I'm a tyke on Momma's

lap. She's slender and dark-haired and brown-eyed and has soft pale skin. I've got a silly tyke grin on my face.

In the middle of one of my dreams I'm waked by a loud noise of some sort. I think maybe Daddy's come home. I git up and peer out my window, which is at the back of the house. Daddy always comes up the back porch. The moon is still near full so I can see all right.

I hear the sound again — a loud thud — against the front of the house. I slip quiet into the livin' room. I look out through a crack in the venetian blinds just in time to see some idjit in the front yard throwin' somethin'.

Somethin' crashes through the window on the other side of the livin' room. Glass flies everywhere.

I jump back.

A brick comes through the other window. More glass flies.

I go runnin' to Daddy's room hopin' he's left his shotgun behind. I see it in the corner, a Winchester double-barrel.

I check the breech and see there's one shell in the left chamber.

I open a drawer at Daddy's bedside lookin' for others. There's not any. I don't have time to scrounge.

I snap the gun closed and take it off safety.

I ease out the back screen door and into the yard and slip around our tumbledown garage. At the corner, under a fig tree where I have a good view of the front yard, I look out again.

I can see okay, enough to see the idjit's still standin' there with somethin' else in his hand. I'm half of a mind to hide and half of a mind to be a Wild Injun.

I decide quick: I step out and fire, well over the idjit's head but not so well that he don't feel a little breeze from the pellets.

The idjit yells he's got a goddam gun and takes off runnin'. Then a car engine revs and a set of headlights come on and I see the idjit jumpin' over our little borrow ditch onto the road. My blood boils and I'm glad I only got one shell 'cause I might be tempted to really shoot the fool. The car comes barrelin' toward the idjit with one door open and the idjit jumps in and the car goes roarin' off, kickin' up clam-shells everywhere. At the first bend, it nearly slides off the road into the bayou.

They're gone cat quick and the night set-tles down again and there's nothin' but the chirp of crickets and a few tree frogs over by the bayou and a thin haze of dust kicked up by the car which looks like fog in the moonlight.

Junior, I just know it.

One thing I'll say about that boy.

He don't give up.

I go back in and go into Daddy's room again. In the moonlight, I rummage more careful for shotgun shells. I find a whole box under what's left of the bed.

I reload the Winchester, both barrels, and go to my room. I lay down and put the gun across my chest with the safety on.

It takes a while to fall asleep.

My bed fills up with gators and Junior and awful things tryin' to git me.

And then I dream that dream again of Momma and Katy and Daddy and me. The same dream, exactly.

16

In the mornin' I wake up and tiptoe to the livin' room barefooted, avoidin' broken glass, which is everywhere. I look out the window and there's a police car pulled up in the driveway.

Daddy's gittin' out of it.

He comes round to the back door as usual.

I say hi, Daddy.

Hello, Meely.

Daddy looks beat as a junkyard car. He's got a small bruise on his chin.

I say did you catch a ride with the police?

One of 'em offered. I didn't want to but otherwise I'd've had to hitch and that could've took a while. They've took my driver's license you see.

Oh.

Actually, they took it some time ago 'cause I won't pay for the tag and I won't git insurance. But a man cain't not drive.

No sir. I guess not.

Daddy closes the back door and runs his

hands through his hair.

He says I went in to persuade 'em otherwise but it didn't go well.

I say I see.

Daddy says I tried to git that fella to show me where in the Constitution it says a man's gotta have a tag and insurance. Nowhere is where.

Daddy shakes his head all disgusted.

He says they wouldn't listen. They took the truck, too. Things got a little hot.

I shake my head disgusted, too.

I say did you fight 'em, Daddy?

He says I'm afraid I did. I guess I could've thought about that a bit beforehand.

Daddy looks at me good for the first time. He says what happened to you, Meely?

I had a bit of a ruckus, too, Daddy.

Boy, it shore looks like you did. Was it one or more?

I say more.

He says how many?

'Bout six.

What do they look like, Meely?

I say some of 'em don't look so good. I had reinforcements.

Who?

Chilly Cox.

Daddy says that big ole Cox boy way up the bayou?

I say that very one.

He says was it that Junior Guidry and that bunch?

I say it was.

Do you want me to go over there?

No sir. I don't think that's necessary.

He says you didn't pick it, did you?

No sir, I didn't.

He says well, okay. I'm glad Chilly was there to help out.

I say me too, Daddy. Anyway, they came back last night throwin' rocks at our window.

Daddy says idjits.

I say they broke two.

Daddy shakes his head, disgusted again.

I say I scared 'em off with your shotgun.

He said did you show it or fire it?

Fired it. Over the main idjit's head.

Daddy says hah! Did they run hard?

I say they pretty near drove their car in the bayou runnin'.

Daddy laughs at this. He says shuh, Meely, I'da give anything to see that.

Daddy looks up at the kitchen ceilin', like he's thinkin' things over. Then he shakes his head.

The world shore is peculiar, ain't it, son?

Yes sir, it is. You want some coffee, Daddy? I'll make some.

I'd love a cup, son. Jail coffee ain't drinkable.

I go rustlin' for a pot under the sink.

Daddy takes a seat at the kitchen table. He unties his boots and takes 'em off. Daddy's got bad feet. He rubs his toes and I see his socks are wore through like mine are.

He says Meely, my business in town didn't go well and the last of that gator money is gone.

I say I'm sorry, Daddy.

He says lucky I went to the store 'fore I left.

I say yes sir, it is. We got plenty of stuff in the cupboard. We ain't gonna starve.

He says well, I better go alligator huntin' again.

Yes sir, I s'pose that's right.

He says you wanna come with me?

I'm surprised as Daddy hasn't axed me to go gator huntin' with him in a while.

I say shore.

He says the only hitch is that we'll have to go to town to git my truck.

I look at Daddy serious. I don't think, what I know of the police, that they'll think this is a good idea.

I say okay, but what about your license?

Daddy shrugs.

I say I thought they took the truck away?

He says yeah, but they didn't lock it up or nothin'. The truck's just over behind the police station in a parkin' lot. They've took the key but I got another.

It's in my toolbox out in the garage.

Won't that 'cause more trouble?

I s'pect I'm in enough already. A little more ain't gonna matter. Besides, I'll just borrow it.

I say borrow it?

Daddy says borrow it. A man cain't very well steal his own truck.

No sir, I guess not. When do you want to go?

Daddy says after dark. We'll hitch into town and git the truck and come back and pick up the pirogue then head over to Bayou Canard. Some ole boy told me he was bulleyein' frogs way back in that marsh a week ago and spied a couple of big gators.

I say okay, Daddy. But what if we git caught at the police station? Won't they have it in for you?

Daddy reaches over and tousles me on the head. He says you worry like your momma, son, which ain't all bad. But don't you worry, Meely. We won't git caught. Nobody watches that parkin' lot.

I'm not as shore as Daddy is about his plans. I fill the pot with water and git down a kitchen match and light the stove. I put the water on to boil and fill up the basket of the coffeepot.

Daddy gits up and walks down the hall to the livin' room and comes back shortly.

He says Meely, them bricks shore is hard on windows, ain't they?

I say they shore are. I'll git some of that leftover plywood in the garage and cover the holes till we can git 'em fixed.

Daddy says well, that oughta work, son. Daddy looks at my face again and says, Meely, one day Junior's gonna really make me mad.

I nod.

I say Daddy, he's pretty much made me that way already.

Daddy sits down at the kitchen table and I pull up a chair on the other side. It wobbles some, as does the table. Things go quiet for a while.

I git up and pour the water into the coffeepot and stand there while it drips slow. Then I pour me and Daddy a cup and take it to the table.

Daddy takes a sip and says that shore is

good coffee, son.

I say thanks, Daddy.

We drink our coffee and then Daddy says he's tuckered out and will take a nap.

I'm stiff and sore and pretty well tired, too.

Daddy goes to his room and then remembers he ain't got no bed. He comes out and goes to stretch out on the sofa.

I go to my room and flop on the bed and I realize I don't mind havin' Daddy in the house.

I lie there and wonder what Daddy woulda done last night.

Shot 'em, I s'pect.

Pretty soon I'm asleep.

17

I wake up and realize I've slept most of the day away. Daddy's stirrin' round in the kitchen. Somethin's cookin', and it's a friendly smell.

I haven't eaten since supper at Cassie's and I'm hungry as a squirrel in winter.

I git up and go see. Daddy's heated up some pork 'n' beans out of a can and cooked up some rice. He's made more coffee. He says you're lookin' a little better, Meely.

I say you too, Daddy, which is true. He's got bags round his eyes but he looks fairly rested.

He says I know we're somewhere 'tween dinner and supper but I was hungry.

I say me, too.

We eat every bit of the beans and rice and a whole loaf of bread. We drink two whole pots of coffee.

I clear the dishes away. I'll wash 'em sometime later.

Daddy says we should git started as there might not be much traffic on this ole road after dark. You don't have to come to town to git the truck, Meely. I can git it myself.

I've decided I wouldn't mind stickin' with Daddy for a bit.

I say I'll come.

We go out to the shell road and sit under an oak and wait. A pickup comes along directly. It's ole Joe Daigle who lives up by Elmore's Store. Daddy gits up and sticks out his thumb. Joe slows down, then stops.

He says where y'all goin', LaBauves?

Clear to town, Daddy says.

Joe tells us to hop in.

Daddy climbs in the cab and I jump in the back. I like ridin' in the open air.

It's about an hour to town. It's not all that far, if you just think about miles, but the road's twisty as it follows the bayou and rough and full of potholes, too. Mr. Daigle's truck ain't much and he takes it slow.

We git there just before dark. I guess Daddy's told Mr. Daigle about gator huntin' 'cause he says hope y'all git some big 'uns. He drives off.

Town's quiet and not many people are about. We walk past a place with a red lit sign out front that says Commercial Cafe. A woman and her little girl are sittin' near the big plate glass window eatin' apple pie, which looks good. I've never eat in a restaurant myself.

We walk round a bit till it's nice and dark and then Daddy turns down the street where the police station is. It's just a little place and there's only one police car parked outside. We walk past and nobody comes out and there ain't nobody on the street.

We go around the block and there's the parkin' lot. Daddy's truck is there, parked facin' the road.

Daddy looks round one more time and says well, let's go. He fetches the key out of his pocket and we hop in.

At first the truck won't crank. Then it coughs and sputters and it seems like the longest minute in the world before it finally catches and starts.

There's a hole in the muffler and it's pretty loud and I figger this will send the police runnin' after us.

But nobody comes.

We drive off without the lights on till we git to Main Street. Then Daddy switches them on and we head back out of town.

Ain't no use tryin' to go real fast. Daddy's truck won't go real fast.

I'm fidgety, lookin' back in the side

mirror, though it's got a big crack in it. I keep thinkin' the police will be after us any minute but we git back to the house okay. We load the pirogue in the bed of the truck and git our guns and bulleyes and a jug of water and drive off for Bayou Canard.

I don't relax till we're way down the bayou and on an oil field road that snakes through the swamp. It's narrow and bumpy and overgrowed with Johnson grass. Cypress trees push right up to both sides and it's like drivin' in a tunnel. Daddy says the oil well that was back in the swamp has been pumped out and hardly nobody comes back here no more.

I s'pect it ain't a place the police could find easy, knowin' what I do about the police. I stop bein' fidgety.

The road ends at a narrow ditch and there's a circular turnout just big enough for the truck. We pull in and unload the pirogue and load up our guns and go paddlin' off down the ditch, which is barely wide enough to fit the pirogue, until it runs into Bayou Canard, which itself runs into the deep swamp. The moon's up and throwin' off a lot of light so Daddy says we'll just paddle with our lights off till we git to the spot where the fella says he saw the gators. Daddy says it's quite a ways and he's glad I'm with him to push the pirogue along.

I say I don't mind, which I don't. It's peaceful out here with the moon shinin' through the trees and grasshoppers sawin' in the reeds and frogs barkin' in the ponds and the slap of our paddles on the water. Now and then a nighthawk will swoop low and go whooshin' by lookin' for supper. Tiny bats flit and chase mosquitoes. Sometimes we just quit paddlin' and sit quiet and listen to the swamp rustle all around us. There's about a million live things in the swamp.

We run upon a small flock of summerin' teal and they barely stir as we paddle easy through 'em. I reach out and touch one of 'em with my hand as we go by and he spooks and squalls at me and flaps off and the rest follow in a big ruckus of wings and quacks. Daddy gits a big kick out of this.

Then the night gits real quiet again.

It takes two hours of steady paddlin' to reach the gator area. It's at a point where the bayou breaks into two branches, one a wide meander goin' south, another a narrow slough headin' west. Daddy says we'll head up the slough about a mile where it runs into a series of ponds. That's where that fella saw the gators. But Daddy says if this is gator country, we should start lookin' right away.

So we switch on our lights and go to work.

I right away spy a big bullfrog and point him out to Daddy, who says catch him, Meely, and put him in that gunnysack 'neath your feet there. A few more of 'em and we'll have dinner tomorrow.

Daddy turns the pirogue toward the frog and eases me in and I catch him easy 'cause I got fast hands. The frog kicks hard in the sack and it thumps up and down once or twice and then settles down. Before long I've caught maybe a dozen frogs, which is pretty close to a mess.

We paddle for a long while and seem to have run out of frogs. There ain't a gator in sight.

Then Daddy whispers there's one, Meely.

I look where Daddy's shinin' his light and see an eye on the water, all lit up.

Daddy whispers he's not very big, five foot I guess. You wanna shoot him?

I say shore. I haven't shot me a gator yet.

He says sit real still and I'm gonna paddle slow. We'll keep our lights on him and when we're about twenty feet away you shoot. Put it in his ear.

I never thought of gators havin' ears, really, but 'course they do.

All right, Daddy. I'll do my best.

There's always a chance that a gator will spook, 'specially ones that have been hunted before or real big ones. But this one lays at the top of the water starin'. When we git in range, I take aim with my rifle and fire.

Plop.

There's a big splash as the gator beats the water with his tail.

Daddy says you got him good, Meely! Paddle hard! We don't want him to sink on us!

We paddle hard and git right up to the gator. He's headshot and swimmin' in a slow crazy circle upside down.

Daddy reaches down and grabs him by the neck one-handed. The gator twitches and goes limp and Daddy hauls him in the boat.

He says that's mighty fine shootin', son.

I throw my bulleye on the gator and look him over good. He's not a monster but he is a fine gator without a mark on the hide, and I've shot him just right.

Daddy says at a buck and a half a foot that's almost a ten-dollar bill you're lookin' at. You done good, son.

I flip him over and count the leeches on the underside. There's seven.

I think I might even try to skin this one since he's on the smallish side. Skinnin' gators is hard work. You ring the hide just below the eyes, then skin down, rollin' the hide off clear down to the tail. Cuttin' the hide away from the hackles on the back is pretty tricky.

Gittin' the leeches off is easy. Sprinkle salt on 'em and they shrivel up into a little ball then die. It's interestin' to watch.

We paddle deeper and deeper into the slough, lookin' hard for another gator, but we don't find one. The Big Dipper moves way down in the sky. Daddy says shuh, maybe that fella was tellin' tales or them gators are just layin' low tonight as they sometimes do. I guess we should turn back as we've got us a good ways to paddle to git back to the truck.

We paddle steady goin' back and after a while come out of the slough and out to the broad bayou and Daddy says suddenly doggone it, Meely, looka yonder!

My light's gone dim but I cast my spot where Daddy's is and there's an eye that looks big as a baseball. The gator turns toward the light and now we see both eyes, about a foot apart.

Daddy says son, that might be the biggest gator I've ever seen. C'mon, let's try to git up real close and I'll give him both barrels with my shotgun.

Daddy's sittin' at the back of the pirogue. He picks up his gun and says you paddle us, Meely. Go in slow and steady.

I paddle slow and silent the way Daddy's showed me, never even raisin' the paddle out of the water. We're pretty close to range and I see the gator's head good for the first time. He's a monster, ten foot or better I'd guess. When we're about thirty feet away, Daddy raises the shotgun and aims but the gator suddenly slips under, without so much as a ripple.

Daddy looks at me and puts up a hand motionin' for me to be still. He whispers don't make a move, Meely. I don't think he's spooked bad. I think he might be back up.

We sit dead still and wait and wait. Daddy's lookin' out one side the boat and I'm shinin' the other. The swamp's gone as quiet as the swamp ever is. The frogs have stopped croakin' and the crickets have stopped sawin'. There's not a breath of wind and what's left of the moon sits egg yellow on the black waters.

Suddenly, I catch the gator's eye again, way over to my left. He's about forty feet away. I whisper over here, Daddy.

Daddy shifts round in the pirogue and catches the gator's eye with his bulleye and whispers hold steady, son, he's kinda far but I'm shootin'. He slips the Winchester off safety and aims and lets go with both barrels, *boom boom.*

The shots thunder across the water and wake up the whole swamp and the recoil darn near knocks Daddy out of the boat and there's a giant commotion in the water where the gator is.

He's hit, Meely! Daddy yells. I got him! Paddle hard!

I'm paddlin' and I hear the snap of the Winchester as Daddy opens to reload.

Doggone, Meely, where are my shells?

I shine the light down by my feet and say well, they must be back by you.

Daddy is suddenly *fâché* and says well, doggone it, they ain't.

I say, okay, here, just take the twenty-two, it's loaded.

Shuh, Meely. That little peashooter ain't gonna finish off this gator. This thing's a monster.

By this time we're up on the gator and I can see he's been hit good but he's thrashin' hard like there's still a lot of fight in him.

Daddy says caw, Lord, son, if this ain't the biggest alligator in South Loosiana and I say it might be, Daddy, and he says well we cain't let him git away from us, git in close.

Okay, Daddy, I will but that gator's not ready to come in the boat yet.

No, son, he shore ain't but if he sinks and dies on us we'll be plumb out of luck.

Daddy puts down the Winchester and picks up his paddle and we go straight for the gator as fast as a pirogue can be paddled.

We're just about on him and he's swimmin' in a circle, jerky like. I see a big wound on the left side of his head. Blood is pourin' out. He comes swimmin' blind right toward us and bumps up hard against the boat where Daddy is and tries to swim on by.

Daddy's dropped his paddle and picked up a big hammer that he keeps in the pirogue to finish gators off. He raises it and realizes he won't be able to knock the gator on the head. So he drops the hammer and reaches over and grabs him by the tail with both hands.

The gator thrashes and halfway lifts hisself out of the water and the spray of this catches me in the face like a wave over the bow.

I yell Daddy, let go!

But Daddy yells back caw, dog, I've got him, Meely! I've got him!

My heart is racin' and I wonder who's got who.

Next I know Daddy's fell out the pirogue and it's rockin' hard and I think I'm goin' over the side, too, and it's a miracle I don't.

I look out and my light's gone dim but I see Daddy in the moonlight. He's about on the back of that gator in a big boil of water.

I yell again let go, Daddy!

And next I know the gator is divin' down, showin' me his tail.

I yell again at the top of my lungs, Daddy, doggone it, let go!

But he don't.

As usual Daddy don't listen.

Daddy don't say a word and before I know it Daddy and the gator are gone in one terrible, giant splash.

18

The night's dead quiet again and Daddy's ripples have disappeared. The face of the moon has fell into the water and lays there, starin'. There's a mosquito buzzin' in my ear and a throbbin' in my head and I'm countin' slow to a hunderd.

I figger if I git to a hunderd and Daddy ain't up, he won't be comin' up, least not for a few days.

Eighty-five, eighty-six, eighty-seven . . .

Ninety, ninety-one, ninety-two . . .

There's a splash behind the pirogue.

I switch on what's left of my bulleye and look.

It's the gator belly-up, a giant white lizard in the moonlight.

Then an arm appears from under water and flops round the gator's neck. Then a second.

I paddle over quick and grab at the left one.

I pull on the arm and it gives and Daddy rises like a ghost from the black deep. His eyes are closed and his face is slack.

I pull harder and Daddy still don't move and I start screamin' Daddy, doggone it! Daddy! DADDY!

Then Daddy's eyes flop open, the left one first, then the right, and, though he ain't exactly lookin' at me, he's lookin'. He's lookin' far away and his face is pale and his hair is swirlin' out from his head and if this were not my daddy I'd say it was somethin' that crawled out of Dead John's graveyard.

Then he gags and about half the water in the swamp spews out of his mouth and it's so terrible I cain't look. So I just hold hard while Daddy coughs and sputters and then finally stops.

He says, I'm okay, Meely. You can let go. I've got it now.

You shore, Daddy?

I'm okay, promise.

I let go. Daddy does a funny little flop with his hands that moves him away from the gator some. Then he lays up on his back in the water and just floats as though a man loungin' in bed. His hands are out wide and I notice he's got a wreath of eel grass around his neck. Finally he says Meely, son, that was close. Real close.

I say Daddy, that wasn't smart.

Daddy don't answer right away.

Then he says maybe it wasn't. Put a rope around this gator's tail then paddle toward that little willow ridge over yonder.

Daddy points to the bank maybe a hunderd feet away.

He says I should be able to get up on that little ridge and step back into the boat. Otherwise, you'll have to tow me to the nearest high ground. Ain't no way of boardin' a pirogue from the water without sinkin' us both.

I say all right, Daddy.

I do and it's the hardest hunderd feet of paddlin' I've done, towin' both Daddy and the dead gator. At the willow, Daddy grabs hold to a root stickin' out of the water and pulls himself hard out on the mucky bank, his feet slip-slidin' under him. Then he just sits down in the mud, and runs his hands through his hair.

Whoa, son, I'm whupped.

Yes sir, well, I can see why.

Just give me a coupla minutes.

Take all the minutes you want to, Daddy.

In a while, Daddy has me toss him the bow rope to the pirogue and he pulls it up on the soft bank. I step out, into the ooze, and Daddy steps in, so he can take the rear seat.

It's a long paddle back to the landin',

'specially havin' to tow that gator. Now that I've seen him up close, I realize he's closer to twelve foot than to ten foot.

Daddy don't say much for a while and then, when he's caught his wind, he says caw, dog, Meely, we've prob'ly caught the biggest gator we'll ever catch. Maybe the biggest one that's ever been caught in these waters.

I say Daddy, we'll shore remember this one.

He says that we will. The only thing I could think about down there is whether he was gonna run us under some big ole log and drown us both. That's what gators do, you know. Drown you 'fore they eat you.

I say is that right?

He says that's right, son. 'Member that if you ever git snatched up by one. If you can kick free, odds are you'll git away.

I say well, I thought he'd taken you down for good.

He says huh, lucky that bayou ain't too deep and is clear of stumps. And lucky he was shot as good as he was shot. He give out first, but not by much.

You were under for a long time, Daddy. I counted to ninety-two and you still wasn't up.

Daddy says well, I just had him round the neck and held on like I was ridin' a big horse. There's a bunch of that eel grass down there and I was feelin' a bit tangled.

I say people don't ride horses under-water, Daddy.

Daddy laughs and says I guess they don't, Meely, and I wouldn't recommend it. But I couldn't stand to see him git away. This gator'll keep us in groceries for a month.

By the time we git back to the truck, daylight is bleedin' through the cypresses. It's all we can do, both of us, to load the big gator in the pickup bed. First we git the head up and then part of the belly onto the tailgate. And then we strain and groan and push till the gator is more or less up in the bed. But there's still a lot of tail hangin' over the edge.

We flop the five-footer in beside him and the five-footer looks like a midget. We load the pirogue in beside the gators and head off back to Catahoula.

I realize for the first time that I'm bone tired, and hungry, too.

It's quite a piece from Bayou Canard to our place and Daddy's truck is runnin' even more ragged than usual. It's all we can do to stay awake. Daddy, a coupla times, veers over to the wrong side of the road.

When we git about a mile away from the house, there's a pop and the truck starts to wobble and the steerin' wheel goes shaky in Daddy's hand and I know right away we've had a flat tire.

Doggone it, Daddy says. Of all times for that tire to give out.

I hop out and see it's the right front, which is good since we can jack it up without havin' to unload the gators. I go to fetch the spare and jack out of the bed. The jack is old and rusty and the spare looks about as bad as the tire that blew.

In fact, when I take it out and bounce it on the road I realize it's as flat as the one on the truck.

Daddy's got out the truck by now and looks at me and says aw, Meely, this is bad luck. I bought a used tire and rim a coupla weeks ago and meant to stick 'em in the truck 'cause I knew that spare was on its last leg. The other one's over in the garage at the house. We'll have to go git it.

I look at Daddy and he looks about as beat as I've ever seen him.

I say Daddy, I'll do it. I guess one of us should stay with the gators.

That's true. Well, if you don't mind,

Meely, I'll sit for a while.

Shore, Daddy. You sit. It ain't that far, anyway.

Tired as I am, the walk home feels pretty good since I've sat cramped in that pirogue all night. I feel like I've got knots in my legs and walkin' loosens 'em up. I walk pretty fast and I guess it don't take more'n fifteen minutes to git home.

I cut off the road across the yard and round the corner of the house and start for the back porch.

It's only then that I notice there's a car pulled way up in our backyard in deep Johnson grass up against the sugarcane field.

It's a police car.

I realize I've noticed this too late when I hear somebody holler that's him, Uncle!

I turn and look over toward the garage.

It's Junior Guidry and a policeman.

The policeman's got a shotgun and he's pointin' it at somethin' near the garage.

The somethin' he's pointin' at is Chilly. His chin's forward on his chest and he's tied up with ropes to a post.

19

Uncle steps out with his shotgun. He's got it in his right hand and says where's your daddy, LaBauve?

I look at Uncle and the Wild Injun rises in me. But I know I need to think clear so I say calm as I can, gone gator huntin', like usual.

Well, where'd you come from?

No place special. I was just roamin' the bayou.

Uncle looks at me as though he's not inclined to believe what I say.

He says it's pretty early to be roamin'.

I shrug my shoulders.

He says well, your ole man stole his truck out of the police yard last night and there's a warrant for his arrest.

I say I don't see how a person can steal his own truck.

Uncle sneers at this. He says I can see you're a smart-ass like your ole man. Anyways, when we catch him this time we'll fix him good.

I cain't hold back. I say is that right?

Well, good luck. The only time y'all ever catch Daddy is when he comes into the police station to give one of you a whuppin'.

Uncle scowls at me and says you talk brave for a little sabine bastid but you won't when we're done with you. We've already took care of your nigger friend there.

He waves the shotgun over in the direction of Chilly and I see Chilly ain't right. He's slumped against the garage with his hands behind him and I know right away he's handcuffed. They've already beat on him pretty good.

I say Chilly, what have they done to you?

Uncle says I haven't give the nigger permission to talk. Junior told me what y'all done to him and it'll be a goddam cold day in hell before a Guidry lets a nigger git away with beatin' up one of our own.

I say Junior's a liar and a coward. Junior and his bunch come to ambush me 'cause of a stupid softball game and Chilly caught 'em. He run the rest of 'em off and he give me the stick Junior had whacked me with and I whacked him back a coupla times. He deserved more. But that's exactly how it happened. If Junior wasn't so chicken, he'd tell you the truth.

Junior looks at me and there's knives in his eyes. He says Uncle, he's a goddam liar. Him and this nigger both jumped me unexpected, like I said.

I just look at Junior disgusted and I don't care about the knives in his eyes. I say Junior I hope a cottonmouth bites you on your ugly ass so it'll match your ugly face.

Junior comes runnin' at me and I'm so mad that I don't care anymore. I figger him and Uncle are gonna kill me anyways so I got nothin' to lose. I juke him hard and then swing as he comes by.

I guess I've juked Junior one time too many and he don't fall for it and slams clean into me, drivin' a knee into my belly.

I feel the wind go outta me and I know my only chance is to fight dirty.

I knee hard at Junior's balls and I git 'em pretty good and he groans loud. Junior's bent over and I go punchin' at his head and connect a few and I see Junior's eyes all wild. But I don't punch real hard is the problem, or not hard enough to take down a mule like Junior.

Then before I know it Uncle's on me. He's a big ole s.o.b., even bigger'n Junior, but he moves pretty fast even with his pot-belly.

I cover up but he whacks me good on the

head with the gun stock.

I fall hard and I'm dizzy and there's a ringin' in my ears and I know the fight's just been knocked out of me.

The last thing I remember is lookin' at poor Chilly. I see his face is puffy and one eye is almost shut and he's got blood on his shirt and he's sayin' somethin' but I cain't really hear.

Then things git dark for a while.

Real, real dark.

20

There's a little light down there under the bayou and it's real pretty. It's movin' slow away from the boat. I figger it's Daddy ridin' that gator. I'm sittin' in the boat with Momma and Katy.

I say look, Katy cher, it's Daddy.

Katy coos and giggles and Momma says I wish he'd come up and I say well, Momma, don't you worry 'cause he always does. I've seen him do it a million times.

Then the light goes out and the bayou turns dark, so dark that I cain't see Momma's face nor Katy's though they're sittin' right next to me in the boat.

I look up in the sky and see a fallin' star. It starts as a dot and gits bigger and bigger and bigger till it's big as the full moon. It plops into the bayou next to the boat and hisses and sinks down deep.

Suddenly everything below is lit up and it's like lookin' into a goldfish bowl and we can see Daddy clear.

Daddy's straddlin' that gator and suddenly behind him is Junior swimmin' real hard. Junior and Roddy and that bunch and Uncle too, all swimmin' after Daddy. Junior's got a knife clenched 'tween his teeth.

I yell real loud, Daddy watch out, but he cain't hear through the water and I see the pack closin' in on him. I yell and yell and yell and suddenly the light goes out.

It's crow black and Katy's cryin' real loud. Katy's screamin' at the top of her lungs.

Next I know, I hear Chilly talkin'. He says Meely, Meely, you all right? Talk to me, Meely. Talk to me.

I open my eyes and I'm still dizzy and I feel like my head's in a gator's jaws and he's chompin' good. And for a second I don't know where I am and half think I'll see Momma and Katy and then realize I've been dreamin'.

I try to git my head up so I can look over at Chilly but it's as heavy as wet cement.

I say I been better, Chilly. How long have I been out?

He says for a while.

I realize I don't see Uncle and Junior. I ax Chilly where are they?

He says in your house, Meely. I think they're bustin' things up. I've heard glass breakin'.

I say what happened to you, Chilly?

He says they got me last night. I was hitchin' back from Cassie's. I thought I was far enough up the bayou not to worry about things. Then this police car pulled up and said they just wanted to ax me a few questions. I went over and one of 'em got out and walked over real slow and then before I know it he's got me shoved up against the car. The other'n jumps out and ole Junior comes out of the cane field. I coulda fought 'em hard, Meely, but I figgered they'd kill my sorry ass if I did. So I didn't. They got me in the car and started beatin' on me real good. I was stupid. Shuh, I shoulda give 'em hell 'cause they prob'ly gonna kill us anyway.

I look at Chilly and realize how bad and tired I feel all over. I'm tied up, too. There's a rope around my wrists and it's lashed to Chilly's handcuffs. I tug on the ropes but they cut into my skin.

I shake my head. I say I'm sorry, Chilly, for gittin' you in this mess.

He says Meely, you didn't do nothin' and you didn't ax me to run Junior and his gang off.

I say well, I shore appreciate it. If we git free of this Junior won't bother us no more. I'll see to that.

171

I cain't think clear about how I'll do this. Truth is, I cain't think much at all. My head is all fuzzy. I tug at my ropes and pain shoots through my wrists again. I think about callin' out for Daddy but if he's still in the truck it won't do no good. And if he's headin' this way, it would just tip off Junior and Uncle.

I hear the back screen door slam and I see Junior and Uncle comin' out. Junior's carryin' somethin'. Uncle's got his shotgun. I see Uncle's also carryin' a couple of bottles of liquor, I guess some Daddy had hid someplace. He takes a sip right out of one of the bottles as they come down the steps and then throws it against the side of the house and it smashes loud.

That's that cheap nigger wine Uncle says, wipin' his mouth. He holds up the other bottle and says now this one ain't bad. Ole Crow. I bet that wino LaBauve was savin' it for Christmas.

Uncle gits a big belly laugh out of this. So does Junior.

Junior comes up to me and shows me what he has in his hands.

He says look at this, Mealy Mouth, it's a pitcher of you and your sabine momma. Uncle says he knew her and she was a whore and she slept with niggers like this one.

Junior points at Chilly.

Junior says ain't that right, Uncle?

Uncle has gone over by the police car to stash the bottle of whiskey away. He says that's right, Junior. She was a whore and this boy's prob'ly got a nigger daddy someplace.

They go to belly laughin' again.

I struggle hard and I don't care if I have to tear my arms off I'm intendin' to git my hands on Junior.

Uncle laughs at me and takes out a cigarette and lights it up. He walks over from the car and blows smoke in Chilly's face then touches the cigarette to Chilly's arm.

Chilly hollers and struggles against the cuffs and I yell goddammit leave him alone! And I realize I've got tears in my eyes and that if I git loose and git my hands on a gun I'll kill both of 'em.

Junior slaps me hard across the face with his free hand and says we don't allow no sabines to talk that way to us, do we, Uncle? Then he says gimme that cigarette here and he throws down the frame that holds Momma's pitcher and stomps on it so the glass breaks.

Then he reaches down and takes the

pitcher out and holds it up and then holds the cigarette to one corner.

He says Mealy Mouth, say good-bye to your momma and he cackles as the edge of the pitcher starts to smoulder.

Then there's a noise off at the edge of the cane field and the smile disappears from Junior's face.

Daddy steps out of the field with the Winchester double-barrel up at his shoulder.

And he says to Uncle, drop that gun or I'll blow your head off.

He nudges the gun Junior's way. He says Junior's head, too.

21

Daddy's less than twenty feet away. He's got a good bead on Uncle and I hear the click of the gun as he takes it off safety and I see Daddy's got a snake-cold look in his eye.

Uncle backs away from Chilly. He puts his hands above his head, holdin' the shotgun up too, but hesitates to drop it.

Uncle says goddammit, LaBauve, you'll git the 'lectric chair if you hurt me. I'm a police officer. We already got warrants for your arrest. You're in enough trouble already.

Daddy jerks the gun hard right and fires one barrel and the rear window of the police car blows up and glass flies everywhere. He says the next one blows your head off. I'm countin' to three.

Daddy says one, two . . .

Uncle lets the gun fall out of his hands and it thumps soft into the high St. Augustine grass.

Daddy comes forward and kicks the gun away and tells Uncle to keep his hands up. Then Daddy knocks him good in the stomach with the butt of the Winchester. Uncle groans and doubles over.

Daddy says lay belly down on the ground and don't make me ax you twice. Uncle does.

He then walks up to Junior, who's too scared to move.

Daddy says hand that pitcher to my boy.

Junior's hands are shakin' and he's turned white.

I'm still tied up so Junior turns and lays the pitcher at my feet. I see it's been scratched and one corner's burnt off but otherwise it's okay.

Daddy says now, apologize to my boy.

Junior looks at Daddy. For just a second Junior looks like Junior usually looks — he looks like he might like to have a go at Daddy same as he likes havin' his go at me.

But Daddy nudges Junior on the shoulder with the barrel of the gun and says cold, Junior, don't make me do anything I'm gonna regret. Now, for the last time, apologize to my boy.

Junior's shoulders go slump and he looks down at the ground.

He says sorry.

Daddy says sorry what?

Sorry I burned the pitcher of your momma.

Sorry what else?

Junior looks at Daddy confused.

Daddy says Junior, what else did you do to my boy? I don't think it's that hard to remember.

Junior shuffles his feet. He says sorry that I hit you.

Daddy shakes his head, disgusted. He says well, you should be 'cause only cowards pick on people half their size.

Then Daddy says now, look at me good, Junior, 'cause there's one more thing you have to be sorry for.

I can tell Junior would like to be done with apologizin' but the fight's gone out of him.

He glances hangdog at Daddy. He says what's that?

Daddy says what was it you called us LaBauves?

Junior looks confused. He stammers well, uh, well . . .

Daddy says all right, Junior, I'll help you. I think you called us sabines. Is that right?

Junior opens his mouth but cain't seem to find any words. Daddy nudges him again with the gun. He says come on, Junior, I don't have all day.

Junior don't need another nudge. He looks at me and says I'm sorry, Meely.

Sorry I call you a sabine.

Daddy looks at me. He says did he say that loud enough for you, son?

I nod my head.

Daddy says you're pathetic and ignorant, Junior Guidry. Now just go over there and lie next to your uncle.

Junior moves that way slow with his hands in the air and as he moves away Daddy plants a foot into his backside and gives him a good hard kick. Junior goes sprawlin' on his face next to Uncle and lies still.

Daddy looks at me and then at Chilly and says which one of these cowards did this to you?

Chilly says both of 'em.

I say Uncle hit me with the gun.

Daddy steps forward to where Uncle is lyin' and gives him a good kick in the ribs and then another and then raises the double-barrel and points it at Uncle's head and says you know, I've about had it with you Guidrys.

He sticks the barrel of the gun right against the back of Uncle's head and that terrible look gits in his eyes again and suddenly the world gits real quiet.

A gnat buzzes soft in my ear and I realize how still the mornin' has become and how

I don't have a voice so I cain't even yell. I want to say no, Daddy, and my mouth moves but no words come out.

I close my eyes and the shotgun explodes and I know that's it, that Daddy has finally done somethin' that cain't be put right.

I realize I have tears in my eyes and I force myself to look up.

I see there's a pretty good hole in the dirt, a foot deep and a foot round, about six inches from Uncle's head.

Daddy has already broken open the breech of the double-barrel and reloaded. He raises his gun and shakes his head all disgusted and says to Uncle gimme the handcuff key.

Uncle I see is shakin' and don't appear to hear so Daddy kicks him again and says the key, now.

Uncle reaches clumsy into his pocket and gits the key and throws it in the general direction toward Daddy. Daddy picks it up and backs up, and with a eye on Uncle unlocks Chilly's cuffs. Then he says to Chilly reach into my pocket and git my knife and cut Meely free.

Chilly does so.

I'm still all woozy and decide to sit down with my back against the garage.

Daddy says Meely, I was wonderin' what

was takin' you so long. What should we do with this barrel of trash we've got here?

I see the cold has gone out of Daddy's eye so I say real loud we should kill Junior and Uncle both as they'll never leave us alone. But I s'pect if we do, we'll git the 'lectric chair.

Daddy nods at me and says you know, Meely, it might be worth a turn in the 'lectric chair to git rid of these two water moccasins. They'll prob'ly try to give us the 'lectric chair anyways as we're LaBauves, so I don't see what we've got to lose. We can always chop 'em up and feed 'em to the gators and nobody'll ever know what happened to 'em.

Chilly says Mr. LaBauve, them two are so ugly and mean that the gators prob'ly won't eat 'em. I'm gonna give both of 'em a good kick and then if you don't mind I'm gonna git outta here. I think I'm done with Catahoula Bayou.

Daddy says well, Chilly, I s'pect we are, too, so you might as well just come with us.

Chilly says maybe I will then.

Daddy says you okay enough to travel, Chilly?

Chilly says okay or not, it don't matter, I ain't stayin' here.

Daddy says you, Meely?

I say I'll be all right, Daddy.

Chilly moves for the first time and I see he's limpin' and he goes over and he kicks Junior good and Uncle, too. Uncle groans loud like and says stop it.

Junior squalls like a baby. He says please don't kill me, please don't.

Chilly says oh just shut up, Junior.

I say Daddy as they're sissies and crybabies, let's just cuff 'em like they had me and Chilly and leave 'em here and by the time anybody comes to see about 'em we could be halfway outta Loosiana.

Daddy says shuh, Meely, you're a better man than me but if that's what you wanna do then let's do it.

He goes over and nudges Junior and Uncle with the barrel of the shotgun.

You two, up against the garage.

They git up slow. Uncle clutches his right side where he's been kicked and Junior walks with his hands over his head.

Daddy tells me to give the cuffs to Chilly and tells Chilly to run the cuffs round an ole post and then lock Uncle and Junior together right wrist to right wrist, then tie their legs to the post, too.

Chilly does.

Junior and Uncle are all trussed up like pigs at a *cochon de lait.*

Daddy says Meely, if you can, run inside and git us a box of groceries that we can carry with us back to the truck. Chilly and I will rustle up that spare.

I say I can manage that, Daddy.

Daddy then walks over to where he's kicked Uncle's shotgun and picks it up and tosses it to Chilly.

He says Chilly, you a hunter?

Yes sir, I am.

Daddy says well, now you've got you a new gun.

Chilly says thank you, I could use one.

Daddy says oh, and one more thing. He takes the Winchester and goes up and shoots out a tire on Uncle's police car. He reaches in his pocket and reloads and shoots out two more. He reloads again and shoots out the last.

Then Daddy opens the car door and shoots out the radio.

He says shuh, I guess they won't chase us with this 'un.

I pick up the pitcher of Momma that's lyin' on the ground then I go in and see about the groceries. Junior and Uncle have made a big mess inside, tearin' everything apart. They've smashed just about every glass and plate there is, not that we had so many.

By the time I'm done, Daddy and Chilly have rummaged round in the garage and got that spare tire. Lucky this one's got air in it.

Daddy says all right, let's go.

Chilly says just give me one minute.

He goes over toward Uncle and Junior, who look at him fearful, and he reaches down. I think he's grabbin' some dirt but I see that instead he's reached down into a red aints' nest and come up with a big double handful. They swarm all over his hands and up his arms and he says, boy, these things sting.

He then walks over and pulls on Junior's waistband and dumps a handful in his pants.

He does the same for Uncle.

I can already hear Uncle cussin' us as we head across the yard and back to the truck. Junior lets out the most pitiful wail I've ever heard.

Goddam you, Junior, I say, but not so loud that Daddy would hear it. Goddam, you deserve it.

22

Back at the truck, I say Daddy, what'll we do with these gators?

He says take 'em with us, son. Someplace safe we'll stop and skin 'em out and their hides will be our runnin' money.

Chilly has got a look at the monster gator for the first time. He says doggone it, Mr. LaBauve, this is the gator to beat all gators.

It shore is, Chilly, even if I did catch it myself.

We git the flat tire changed. Daddy turns the truck around and we head on off back toward the way we come. Daddy figgers if we can git up to Yankee City before anyone comes after us, we can find some back roads all the way to Texas.

Myself, I ain't never been very far off of Catahoula Bayou and I worry about this ole truck makin' it twenty miles down the road, much less Texas. But I don't say so. We've got plenty to worry about already.

I realize I was worryin' about the wrong thing 'cause we ain't driven six miles when behind us, comin' up fast on the shell road, is a police car, lights flashin'. Then they switch on a siren.

I yell doggone it, Daddy, some of Uncle's friends are right behind us!

Daddy looks in his rearview mirror and spies the police car and says y'all hold on. I ain't in favor of bein' caught just yet.

I say Daddy, we cain't run in this ole truck.

He says well, Meely, it's the only thing we've got to run in.

Daddy guns the Dodge and she sputters and backfires and picks up a little speed. Pretty soon we're doin' fifty or so on the shell road and kickin' up a storm of chalky white dust. Pretty soon sixty, which is about all the truck will go. I can hear the engine whinin' and we're wobblin' pretty bad.

Daddy moves to the center of the road, which is dangerous 'cause this road ain't nothin' but a bed of clam shells heaped up real loose between the ruts, and I can feel that the truck just wants to slide out from under us.

But Daddy says them ole boys gonna eat a lotta dust before they git us.

Pretty soon the police are fishtailin' right behind us but the road's too narrow for them to git around and cut us off and half the time they disappear under the dust cloud.

When I look back, I notice the one who's not drivin' has a shotgun and he's tryin' to poke hisself out the window for a shot. But there's dust and shells flyin' everywhere and the car's slidin' bad and he's havin' a hard time holdin' an aim of any kind.

I look ahead and before I know it I see we're comin' up to the Waterproof Canal bridge, which is only one lane.

And then suddenly there's a truck comin' right at us over the bridge.

I yell watch it, Daddy!

I look at Daddy and he grips the wheel with both hands and brakes hard and then yells I see him, Meely!

He brakes hard and yells Lord, boys, I don't know if I can hold her and then we lose it completely.

The truck starts to spin on the shells and we go around once and then once again. Everything gits quiet and I'm watchin' the world spin in slow motion.

I'm pitched halfway out of my seat lookin' back and I see the police car come speedin' right up to us, slidin' sideways, too, in a hurricane of dust and shells and why we haven't rammed each other I don't understand.

They've slid so close to us that I can see the face of the driver through the dust and I can see a wild look in his eyes.

Suddenly, I know why, for as we fishtail around again, I see the big gator's been flung out the truck and is sailin' through the air.

It sails in a dark cloud like some big black dragon through the dust and flyin' shells and the noise and it lands hard on the hood of the police car.

It lands hard and flies up again and then goes crashin' through the windshield headfirst and makes a terrible smashin' sound.

Then I hear Chilly yellin' and Daddy sayin' hold on we're goin' over and then the world is tumblin' upside down again and again and again.

And that's all I remember, till the next thing I know we're all smashed together in the truck, which is lyin' on its side in the cane field.

23

There's a horsefly buzzin' round my head and my right leg's hurtin' bad. I'm at the bottom of the pile and bein' half smothered by the weight of Chilly and Daddy. There's a crazy sound and I realize it's the wheels still spinnin'. The engine's on and we're still in gear. This ole truck is tougher than I thought it was.

Daddy somehow manages to untangle his arm from behind Chilly and shuts off the motor and things git quiet and he says why ain't we all dead?

Chilly says I don't know. Are you shore we're not?

I say my leg's hurt bad, Daddy, and I'm bein' squashed.

Daddy says well, lemme try to git out of this thing, son.

He reaches up and pulls himself through the open window so that he's now sittin' on the door. He offers Chilly a hand and Chilly grabs on to the window frame and climbs out, too.

Chilly's all stiff and I see him walkin'

round the front of the truck. He says Mr.
LaBauve, let's you and me see if we can
push this thing over.

Daddy looks pale and beat. He says
Chilly, I don't think even you are that
strong.

Chilly says maybe I'm not. But let's try.

Daddy hops off and goes around and
they put their backs to the truck. I sit still,
my leg burnin', and feel the truck tilt back
and forth and Chilly gruntin' and sayin'
come on you ole mothuh, move. Then
Daddy yells push hard and she goes over
and rights herself with a big groan of
springs and axles.

Daddy says man, oh man, Chilly, I take
that back. He tries to open my door but
it's stuck so he comes around the other
side and opens the driver's door and pulls
me out by gittin' his hands round my
chest.

Daddy lifts me, then puts me careful on
the ground with my legs out and my back
against the truck.

Daddy then feels my leg between my
knee and ankle and says Lord, son, I think
you've might've broke it.

I say maybe I have, Daddy, 'cause it
shore does feel bad.

We then look around for the first time.

There's dust everywhere. We see the police car turned sideways across the road about thirty yards away with that big gator stuck like an arrow halfway through the middle of the windshield. There's steam pourin' out from under the hood. The driver of the car is slumped over the wheel. We cain't even see the other officer.

Daddy looks at me. He says Lord, son, what a mess.

He walks over and looks in and shakes his head. I hear him say a word or two to those policemen though I cain't make out what the words are. He walks back to us and says them fellas been banged around pretty good.

I say they're not gonna die are they, Daddy?

I wouldn't say so, Meely. But they've got some hurtin' to do.

We'd forgot about the other truck comin' at us over the bridge when we hear a voice sayin' boy, LaBauve, that was a damned close call.

Of all people, it's Francis Hebert, Joey's daddy. I look back down the road and see his pickup with his left wheels canted halfway into a ditch.

Daddy looks at Mr. Hebert and says yes it was.

He says y'all in some kinda trouble.
LaBauve?

Daddy says none that we picked. But
there's them ole boys there and a coupla
more at the house who need tendin' to.
You might wanna fetch help.

He says I guess I better. What about
your boy?

Daddy says broken leg I'd guess. He
needs help, too.

Mr. Hebert looks at me. You gonna be
okay, son?

Yes sir. I think so.

He says you wanna come with me,
Emile?

I realize I don't wanna have to explain
any of this to Francis Hebert. I say no sir.
I'll wait here with Daddy.

Daddy says Francis, I'd 'preciate you
gittin' to a phone and callin' the authorities 'cause we cain't hang around too
long.

Mr. Hebert looks at Daddy and says a
man shouldn't run from his problems,
LaBauve.

Daddy says I wouldn't if I had a choice.
But they've got it in for us and now they're
even beatin' on my boy.

Mr. Hebert shakes his head puzzled. He
says well, you ain't goin' nowhere in that

truck the way it looks. You've blown two tires.

Daddy looks back at the truck and shakes his head and says well, we cain't stay.

Mr. Hebert shrugs. Well good luck, LaBauve.

He drives away and Daddy says we better git and I say Daddy, I cain't git. I know my leg's broke, and I'm too tired to git.

Daddy kneels down beside me and rolls up my right pants leg. My lower leg is twisted in a funny shape and is already turnin' black and blue.

He says we'll carry you, Meely. I just cain't leave you here, son.

I say then none of us will git far. Anyway, I wanna stay and tell our side.

Daddy looks at me and I can tell he doesn't think much of this idea.

He says they'll never believe you, son. Not in a million years.

I say they prob'ly won't but the truth's the truth and anyway they won't put a boy in the 'lectric chair.

Daddy says maybe not, Meely, but they've really got it in for me now and if they don't have me they'll just be hard on you instead. I know — I've been leaned on a few times. It's not right that you should have to stay behind and face that.

Daddy rises and looks around, like he's lost and tryin' to find his bearings. He looks back at me and says I'm sorry, Meely. It might be better just to stay and face this, but I just cain't. I'm all done with jail. I wouldn't last long in there this time.

I say Daddy, I know that. I want you to go — go, and take Chilly, too. They'll be a lot rougher on you two than me.

Daddy says well, Meely, you're shore somethin'.

Thinkin' about this, I'm not shore what I am.

So I say shuh, I'm a LaBauve, Daddy. 'Member we've got the Wild Injun in us.

I'm not shore this is how I really feel. I'm hopin' Mr. Hebert has fetched an ambulance and it comes pretty quick but not so quick that Daddy and Chilly cain't slip away.

Daddy smiles a tired smile. He says we shore do, don't we?

Chilly says Meely, if you see Cassie you tell her I'm okay.

I say I will, Chilly.

Daddy looks around confused for a minute then sees somethin' big layin' over about thirty feet from the truck.

It's the pirogue. It's landed in the cane patch and don't seem to have a scratch on it.

He says Chilly, we've got some luck. You git that pirogue and I'll fetch the paddles and our guns from the cab. We're right at the Waterproof Canal. The edge of the Catahoula Swamp is a mile's paddle. I know that swamp good. I know how to git us good and lost.

Chilly goes and lifts the pirogue over his head with two hands like he's pickin' up a two-by-four. He walks toward a line of hackberries that mark the bayou. Daddy follows and helps Chilly slip the boat into a little clearin'. Chilly edges into the front. Even from where I am, I can see the pirogue is sittin' awful low in the water. But it floats, which is all that matters.

Daddy puts his hands on the pirogue's back rail and, with one foot in the boat, pushes off with the other. The pirogue glides toward the middle of the bayou.

Daddy turns and waves his paddle at me.

Take care, Meely.

I will, Daddy.

When things cool off and I git settled someplace, I'll come for you.

I know you will, Daddy.

Daddy says Chilly, can you use a paddle?

Chilly says no but I can learn.

Daddy takes a deep stroke on the right side of the boat and they paddle off to God knows where.

24

I've been in jail twelve days now in what they call juvenile lockup. Uncle and Junior told their lies like I figgered they would. So after they carried me to the hospital and put a cast on my busted leg, they took me off to jail.

A few days later I had a 'rainment or some such. They took me before a judge and there was this lawyer who looked sleepy and yawned all the time and axed me whether I wanted to plead innocent or guilty, it didn't matter to him.

I said well, since I hadn't done nothin' wrong and had only defended myself, maybe innocent would be best. He said suit yourself, kid. There was some business with the judge and the lawyer said to the judge that after the 'rainment he was too busy to do anythin' else for me. The judge said okay so I've sat since.

I'm up for 'tempted murder plus a bunch of other stuff. Assault and destruction of police property and such. So is Chilly. As for Daddy, the jailer says they've throwed the book at him, whatever that means. The jailer acts like it's a pretty big book — prob'ly about the size of the Bible. New and Old Testament.

Mr. Hebert fetched help pretty quick. When they come to git me, I wouldn't leave the truck till somebody went and found them poor frogs I'd caught and let 'em go in the bayou. Funny what you git upset about sometimes.

But I suddenly knew what them frogs felt like.

My leg was broke in two places but clean so the doctor says I'll mend quick.

First one sergeant then a captain come and axed me all kinds of questions. I tell the same story every time, the true one.

I tell 'em if Daddy was a bad man Junior and Uncle would be dead now stedda runnin' round tellin' lies.

I tell 'em it's true Chilly put red aints down Junior's and Uncle's pants but all things considerin' he coulda done worse.

Captain Landry — he's one of 'em in charge of me — seems to git a kick out of that part of the story. I guess that's another part that Junior and Uncle hadn't told.

I ax Captain Landry what's happened to our gator? He says well, it got all cut up when it went through the windshield of that police car. So the hide was pretty well ruint and the Wildlife and Fisheries came and took it away. But he said it was so big they were thinkin' about stuffin' it and puttin' it in a museum somewhere up over by Baton Rouge.

It seems a shame. I tell Captain Landry how Daddy shot that gator then jumped in the water and wrestled him up like he did. I'm not shore he believes me but he laughs and says Meely, I've never seen a bigger gator no matter how y'all caught it.

Sergeant Picou, he's the other one who axes me questions. He's heard the stories about the gator and the red aints, too, but he don't laugh. He's dark and bald and got oily skin and smells like cigarettes and sometimes like liquor. I s'pect he might be a good friend of Uncle's.

I say it's true that Daddy did go and take his truck from the police station and how we went gator huntin' after. I tell 'em what Daddy says about the Constitution and how it don't say nothin' about a man needin' insurance or a driver's license. I say I'd prob'ly git insurance and a license if I was ever to go to drivin' but it ain't how Daddy feels.

They always ax me if I know where Daddy and Chilly are as though Daddy's got one particular hideout in the swamp. I say what I always do, which is that they run off toward the swamp and that's the last I saw of 'em.

I don't tell 'em about the pirogue, which I figger messed up their search a bit. Captain Landry told me they went swarmin' all over those fields and woods with men and dogs and thought shore they'd catch 'em.

They shoulda brought a boat.

I keep tellin' the police if they ain't found 'em yet, they won't unless Daddy wants to git found.

Sergeant Picou sometimes comes in by hisself and gits all mad when I say that. He says it's lucky nobody got killed in that wreck as they would've shore give Daddy the 'lectric chair if they had. He said had that gator smashed through the windshield just a foot to the left, it woulda taken one of those police officers' heads off. He says it's bad enough as those policemen were in the hospital for several days. He says it's lucky Uncle and Junior didn't die of heatstroke 'cause we'd left them tied up in the sun. He says we're all in a bunch of bad trouble. He says if I cooperate they might go easy on me and if I don't they'll send me to reform school for a long time.

He says anyway, LaBauve, why would

you bother protectin' your ole man when he run off like a coward and left you holdin' the bag like he did?

Sergeant Picou knows when he says this it gits my goat. He says no matter what, when they catch your ole man they'll have him bustin' rocks up at Angola Prison.

I tell Sergeant Picou I've cooperated as much as possible. I say Daddy run off 'cause he knew Junior and Uncle would lie and he's done give up on jail. I say Daddy wanted me to go with him, but I stayed behind 'cause I wanted to tell our side.

I ax him what they woulda done if poor Chilly and me had got heatstroke after Junior and Uncle tied *us* up.

Sergeant Picou just looks at me disgusted when I say that.

Sometimes he threatens me. He says kid, there's a big fat queer in the men's cell just up the hall and one night I'm gonna give him the key and let him in here at you. You keep bein' a smartass with me and it will happen, I guarantee. You better tell me the truth, boy.

He says do you know what a queer would do to a boy like you?

I say I do but I don't really.

But knowin' Sergeant Picou, I prob'ly wouldn't be in favor of it.

I just look at Sergeant Picou and think about givin' him the Evil Eye, though I ain't yet. I just say all I've told is the truth.

I've had one visitor, Miz Lirette from school. She come to see me when I first got in and has been back pretty much every day. She says Emile, I'm sorry about your leg and all this trouble you're in. She says she knows how Junior has been after me and she's told this to the police and hopes it helps. She says she's lookin' into gittin' me a lawyer.

I say well, I hope you can find one better than that fella at the 'rainment.

She laughs when I say that.

She says she's sorry about Daddy and knows how worried I must be.

I say I am but they won't catch Daddy, no way.

She says well, between you and me, I hope they don't.

Some days I wouldn't mind seein' Cassie.

And Joey, too.

And even crazy ole Chickie Naquin. We could laugh about that cow and talk about heaven and such.

I've got plenty of time to talk here. Nothin' but time.

But nobody else comes.

25

It's mornin' and I'm sittin' lookin' at a magazine that Captain Landry's brought me. It's called *Life* and there's pitchers of movie stars and a princess from some such place. The princess is pretty and it wouldn't be too hard to start thinkin' about heaven, even though I doubt a princess does such things as that.

I'm glad I'm not thinkin' about heaven 'cause I look up and see Miz Lirette has come to my cell door with a man. The jailer lets them in.

She says hi, Meely, I've brought somebody to see you. This is Mr. Alphonse Dorsey, a lawyer in town.

I say hello. Pleased to meet you.

Mr. Dorsey is an older man, tall and serious as church, with a gray suit and gray hat. His shoes is black and nice and polished and he's got on a stiff white shirt and the prettiest tie I've ever seen. His hair's gone gray along the sides.

He says hello, Emile. Can we talk?

Shore I say.

He and Miz Lirette take a seat on a small wooden bench. Mr. Dorsey takes off his hat and puts it in his lap. He says Miz Lirette here called to ask me to look into your case. I have and I was wondering if I can ask you some questions?

Well, Mr. Dorsey, I'm about axed out, but go 'head.

He goes over the usual stuff and I tell him what I know, even the parts about the Evil Eye and tellin' Junior he will strike out and callin' him ugly as a possum's butt and such. I don't leave nothin' out 'cept how Daddy and Chilly escaped in the pirogue. Mr. Dorsey keeps noddin'.

When I'm finished he says have they been treating you okay, Emile?

Well, 'cept for how sour Sergeant Picou keeps tellin' me how they might git me for 'tempted murder and how he thinks I'm not tellin' the truth, they've been okay. I say I was wonderin', Mr. Dorsey, if Sergeant Picou might be good friends with Uncle. He shore seems partial that way.

Mr. Dorsey looks at me serious and says Emile, whether Sergeant Picou knows Uncle well would be something worth finding out.

Well, if you ax me I think they're the same kind of fella.

Mr. Dorsey nods.

I say I don't even mind the food though those poor men down the hall in them other cells are always complainin' about how bad it is. The cook for the jail must be against salt and pepper and Tabasco sauce. But other'n that he cooks all right.

Mr. Dorsey says how's your leg, Emile?

I say gittin' better. The doctor has come a few times and told me it was mendin' good.

Mr. Dorsey says Emile, I think I'll take your case. Now and then the judge asks us to serve pro bono. Do you know what that is?

I say no sir.

He says well, it's when a lawyer works for people who don't have the money to pay a regular lawyer.

I say Mr. Dorsey, that pretty much describes me. I do have thirty-five dollars tucked away in the house if Junior and Uncle didn't steal it, and I would be happy to pay that to start with if I could git it.

Mr. Dorsey shakes his head and says I think we'll let you hold on to the thirty-five dollars for now. At any rate, Emile, I don't want to mislead you. The charges they've brought against you are serious and if you were convicted they could send you away to reform school. The district attorney, in fact, is of a mind to try you as an adult, which means you could be sent to a regular prison, but I don't think that will happen.

The sendin' me away part, 'specially to a grown-up prison, don't sound so good.

Mr. Dorsey says so we're gonna do a little investigating of our own. And at some time or another, hopefully not too long from now, you'll have to go before a judge again and tell him what you know just like you've just told me. But there's a good chance when the judge hears all this, he'll dismiss the case.

I say what about Daddy and Chilly?

He says Emile, that's a different matter and will be dealt with when they're found. Truth be told, their running from the law is against them. Even if your father had a good reason to do what he did to Junior and Uncle, he's still got a problem about taking his truck when the police told him not to. Plus shooting up that police car. Plus taking that officer's shotgun.

I say what happens if they never git found, Mr. Dorsey?

He shakes his head serious again and says that the law has an awfully long arm and people who've run for years and years still get caught.

I have a funny thought in my head — Daddy bein' chased by a bunch of policemen with long skinny arms. I still cain't think such arms would do the police much good.

Mr. Dorsey says oh, and one other thing, Emile. Even if we get you out of this mess the state is going to try to put you in an orphanage.

I say whatever for?

Because your daddy's on the run and even if he weren't the state would argue that he's an unfit parent.

I say unfit?

He says that means he doesn't take proper care of you, Emile.

I have to think about this. Compared to other daddies I s'pose Daddy ain't around as much as most. But bein' around ain't everything there is to a daddy.

Mr. Dorsey continues. Do you know, Emile, that your father's been arrested several times on drunk and disorderly charges?

Yes sir, I s'pect he has.

And that the people with the state who decide whether boys should go to an orphanage or not believe your father is an alcoholic?

Yes sir, I know Daddy does drink more than he should.

Well, Emile, it's more serious than that in their eyes. They believe your father is guilty of neglect.

It bothers me that people think this of Daddy but Daddy *is* a hard person to explain. Bein' gone might be all Daddy can figger out to do.

I say Mr. Dorsey, I know Daddy's got some of the Wild Injun in him. But Daddy's never been mean to me. Shuh, he's never even spanked me once, though he fusses me sometimes. And he's taught me an awful lot. Daddy's got a lot of problems but I s'pect the main one is that he ain't got Momma no more.

Mr. Dorsey goes quiet for a while. Then he says well, I have to be honest with you, Emile, it doesn't help any that you don't go to school regularly.

I say I guess I don't. But Mr. Dorsey, I might if I thought it would keep me out of the orphanage.

Mr. Dorsey smiles a little for the first time. He says well, that's good to know, we'll see what we can do. But I just wanted to be honest with you. That's important, Emile. You must always tell me the truth and I'll do the same.

I say that sounds like somethin' Daddy says. I believe Daddy does try to tell the truth, though he might get mixed up about what the truth is.

Mr. Dorsey nods and says I'll be back to see you tomorrow.

He gits up and shakes my hand, which is pretty much the first shake I think I've had. Miz Lirette comes over and hugs me and says take care of yourself, Emile.

I promise I will. I say tell Joey hello for me. Chickie, too. And Miz Breaux, of course.

She says she'll do so.

26

At night when they turn out the lights the jail gits dark and lonesome. There's a bunch of cells up the hall where there must be eight or ten men. I guess one of 'em must be the big fat queer Sergeant Picou told me about.

I hope he stays where he belongs.

The men are s'posed to stop talkin' after lights out but it ain't late, maybe nine-thirty, when they shut the lights off, and some don't stop talkin'. I hear 'em in low voices.

There's one whose name I know 'cause the jailers call him ole Bill. He come in drunk and loud about a week ago. Since then he don't have much to say 'cept now and then he'll say oh Jesus I need a drink or oh Jesus come cut ole Bill loose from this godforsaken place. Oh Jesus, oh Jesus.

When ole Bill sleeps he moans and cries out oh Jesus and sometimes I hear him cryin' and he says oh momma, momma, momma.

They say growed men ain't s'posed to

cry but I know why they do.

I sleep with that pitcher of Momma next to my pillow. I managed to pull myself up on one leg and fetch it out of the truck before they come to take me away and hid it in my pants. Captain Landry saw it one day and said it was okay that I had it. He said Momma was a pretty woman, which she was.

I dream of Cassie a lot. It's funny 'cause I don't really know much about Cassie. I have a hard time even rememberin' exactly what she looks like, 'cept in my dreams. It's usually a dream that has somethin' to do with heaven and that's okay. I figger it's about as close to heaven as I'll git for a while.

I wouldn't mind a supper of barbecued coon, either, or maybe a *sauce piquante* or a gumbo like me and Daddy make. Sergeant Picou says people in jail ain't got no right to expect nothin'. He says it's lucky they feed us at all.

It figgers he'd think that.

I think about Daddy and Chilly. Daddy can live easy in the swamp but I wonder whether Chilly can. I hope Chilly likes fish 'cause I figger they're eatin' a lot of fish. Prob'ly some *choupique* — back in the swamp sometimes them *choupique* is all you can catch. They're prob'ly eatin' rabbit, too. Maybe even possum, though Daddy don't like it. I don't neither. I've skinned a few possums and I might not ever skin another. Even skinned fresh they smell like the second day of a dog layin' dead on the road.

Most times I think I'll see Daddy again but sometimes I wonder if I ever will. Sometimes I half hope he'll come bustin' in here tryin' to git me out and other times I'm afraid he will. If Daddy comes in here tryin' to bust up the police this time, they'll make it real bad for him. I know that for a fact.

I hear somebody comin' down the hall slow. I know this ain't right 'cause after lights out nobody comes in here unless there's a new prisoner. When that happens, they turn the lights on and wake everybody up.

I sit up on my cot thinkin' it must be that fat man and I feel the Wild Injun rise in me. Still, I don't know what I'll do if it's him.

Fight hard, I guess. I cain't run.

I look and see.

It's Sergeant Picou standin' at the bars. He switches on a flashlight. He's got a funny look on his face, which is all shadowy behind the flashlight beam.

He says whispery LaBauve, I'm not s'posed to tell you this but they fished a body out of the south end of the Catahoula Swamp this afternoon.

At first I don't know what he's gittin' at.

He says it was pretty eat up by gators and crawfish. But it's a white man about fittin' your daddy's description. Same height and build.

My heart about stops beatin'.

He says they're comin' over pretty soon to take you to the hospital to look at the body, see if you can identify it.

He stops and then shines the light directly in my eyes and then away. He says odds are it's your ole man. I guess he's not so good at hidin' after all.

I cain't find my voice right away.

He says we'll prob'ly find that nigger the same way. I'm only sorry that gators got your daddy before we could lock him up in the penitentiary with a bunch of bad ole niggers, yeah buddy. There's some bucks up there at Angola that'd take the piss and vinegar out of him, for shore.

I look at Sergeant Picou and wonder what he's got against me.

Same thing as Junior does, I guess.

I say well, if it's Daddy I'll know. And if

it's Daddy all I can say is that he'd've never been found by the likes of you.

Sergeant Picou takes a bar of my cell in one hand and says you're a smart-aleck little sabine bastid, LaBauve, but now you ain't got no daddy and even if they don't send you to reform school you'll go to an orphanage for shore. You'll be in there with the rest of the little bastids they've throwed away.

I say I'll run away before that happens.

He says you'll run but they'll catch you just like your ole man.

A scream rises in my head and then it just pours out. I yell at Sergeant Picou y'all never caught Daddy! Maybe a gator could but somebody as sorry as you never could — all the deputies in Catahoula Parish couldn't catch Daddy!

Sergeant Picou shakes his light at me like a pointy finger and says you're a smartass now, but you won't be for long, boy. We've got your sorry ass now.

I stand up even though it's hard on my bad leg and hobble over close to Sergeant Picou but not so close that he can grab me through the bars.

I say look at me good.

He says I'm lookin' at you and I don't see much of nothin'.

I give him a double Evil Eye, spinnin' the right eyeball first and then the left one. Then I spit as hard as I can.

A gob catches Sergeant Picou on the chin.

I say the LaBauve *gris-gris* on you, bastid Picou. If my daddy's really dead his ghost will come and stick a butcher knife in you one night. Buzzards will peck out your guts. Maggots will come and eat out your brains.

I cuss him in Cajun like I've learned up at school: *Maudit fils de garce! Fils de putain! Chu de cochon!*

Sergeant Picou staggers back a step and his face is all mad and twisted and then he hollers goddam you, boy, goddam you! Don't you pull that *gris-gris* shit on me! Goddam you!

And then he charges at me, flingin' himself against the bars and reachin' through as far as he can. His flashlight clatters to the floor.

I stumble back, and he gits a hand on my shirt but a button gives way and I fall loose. I'm glad the bars are between me and him, and I'm gladder still when I hear footsteps.

The lights go on and suddenly Captain Landry is at my cell door.

He says Picou, what the hell are you doin' here?

Sergeant Picou just glares at me.

Captain Landry says git the hell out of here right now before I write you up.

Sergeant Picou backs away but he's as angry as I've seen a man. He says that boy is evil! That boy's got the devil in him!

He backs away slow and then almost runs down the hall.

Captain Landry looks at me curious. Did he tell you, Meely? About the body we've found?

Yes sir.

Will you come with me to look at it?

I say I'm shore it's not Daddy but I'll come.

He says they say the body's a mess and you're the only one who might know.

I say don't matter what kind of mess. If it should turn out to be Daddy, I'll know.

He says I'm real sorry to have to do this to you, son.

I feel sick to my stomach. I think I might throw up.

I've said that to Captain Landry — that I don't think it'll be Daddy. But I don't feel as shore as I sounded.

27

I'm still on crutches so we make our way slow down the hall of the jail. We walk by the other cells. One or two men say hey, Meely, or hey, kid, as we go by. I don't know how they know my name but I say hey, fellas, back. I don't see any big ole fat man. I figger Sergeant Picou was lyin' to me.

The jail sits atop the courthouse and we take a creaky elevator down to the bottom floor. It stops and Captain Landry slides open an accordion door and points the way. I see double doors leadin' to steps outside. I hobble through them into the muggy night.

It's the first time I've been out since they put me in jail and the fresh air might feel good 'cept for where I'm goin'.

Captain Landry points to his police car. It's just a regular white car with a blue light on the dashboard. I make my way down a set of steps and git in. This is my third ride in a police car, countin' the one that brought me to the hospital and the one that carried me from the hospital to the jail. I guess I might be catchin' up with Daddy in police car ridin'.

The hospital's not far — nothin' in this town is. It's a big white buildin' with columns out front and a big circular driveway where they drop people off. 'Cause we're in a police car we git to park right at the front door.

Captain Landry says we're goin' up on the third floor. It's a place we call the morgue.

I say what exactly is a morgue?

He says it's a place they bring dead people so they can identify them or examine them.

I say is there more than one body up there?

He says no, son, just one.

I say okay.

The hospital smells funny to me. Like alcohol and such. There's a white wooden desk with a woman talkin' on the phone and a few people sittin' on soft chairs. Most are readin' magazines. A few are starin' out, tired. I figger they all got sick kin, which is a shame.

We walk toward an elevator and a sister stops us. She's in her habit, which I know about 'cause Momma used to bring me to the little Catholic church down Catahoula.

She was plenty friendly with some of the sisters down there and I got to know 'em, I guess. I can remember what they looked like but not their names. It seems so long ago.

The sister says hello, Captain.

Hello, Sister Theresa.

And who do we have here?

Sister, this is Emile LaBauve. He's been with us in juvenile lockup for a while.

Oh. Is there trouble?

I'm afraid there has been.

Is it serious, Captain?

I'm afraid so.

Is he here for his leg?

No, it's about that body they brought in earlier.

Not a relative I hope?

We're afraid it might be his father.

She looks at me and says oh, Emile, I'm quite sorry.

I say I am, too, Sister. But maybe it's not him.

She says was your father a Christian, Emile?

You mean is he?

Yes, of course — is he. We mustn't assume the worst.

I have to think about this a second. Then I say maybe he was though he never talked about it. He wasn't much on church but Daddy's not much on a lot of things. But Momma was for shore. She went to church regular, what I remember.

And where is your mother, Emile?

Dead.

Ah, God called her. Long ago?

I was seven then.

Well, Emile, we can only suppose that God needed her more than we did.

I say for what? I needed her pretty much. Daddy, too.

She looks at me curious like. She says that isn't a question anyone but God can answer.

Well, maybe you could ax him for me. I wouldn't mind knowin', actually.

Sister Theresa shakes her head. She says I don't think it works that way, child. As they say, God works in mysterious ways.

I wonder who it is that says that. But I don't say so.

Sister Theresa pats me on the head.

She says Emile, if your father is dead, we can only hope that he found God before he died.

This sounds funny to me. I say I s'pect Daddy could find God if God is to be found. Daddy can track most anything.

I tell her how Daddy tracked me after Momma died.

She shakes her head and looks at Captain Landry. She says remember, God loves all of his children. If that is your father, I pray that he is with God in heaven.

I'm tempted to say that Daddy has found heaven once or twice but I don't think we'd be talkin' about the same thing. So I don't say nothin'.

She smiles sweet and says would you like me to go with you up there?

I say no thank you.

She bends down and looks me eye to eye. She says God will help you be a brave young man. She closes her eyes and crosses herself and says a prayer and such. She pats me on the head again and walks on down the hall.

We git in the elevator and ride up. It's slow as winter syrup. At the top, the elevator makes a whirrin' noise and opens. There's a hall with a dim light and a man in a white coat standin' down by a closed door.

Captain Landry points toward the man and says that's Paul Comeaux, the coroner.

I say what's that?

He says a doctor who checks into how people died.

I think I wouldn't like such a job.

The coroner walks over and shakes Captain Landry's hand. He says hello, son, I'm Dr. Comeaux.

I say hello.

He says I appreciate you comin'. This shouldn't take long.

I say no sir. I hope it won't.

He says try not to be scared. The body is in pretty bad shape.

I say yes sir. I've heard.

He says we did an autopsy to try to determine how he died.

I say what's that?

He says an operation more or less.

I say did you find out how he died?

Dr. Comeaux says my opinion is that he drowned first — then the gators got him. There's not much face left — the crawfish got at it pretty bad — and gators got most of one leg but there might be other characteristics, hair or other things, that you might recognize.

I say well, Daddy has dark black hair. What about this body?

He says the same.

I say Daddy had dark eyes.

He says son, there's only one eye left and

it's pretty shot. But it's definitely dark.

I swallow hard.

I say all right, well, I should have a look.

He says son, I have to warn you the smell is pretty bad. This person has been dead a few days.

Yes sir. I understand.

Do you want a handkerchief?

No thank you.

Dr. Comeaux pauses, then says you better take one anyway. If you need to throw up, it's okay. I have grown men in here who keel right over sometimes.

Yes sir.

He gives me the handkerchief. It's white with blue initials sewed on it.

We walk together down the hall to the door. Dr. Comeaux opens it. There's a big hooded white light hangin' from the ceilin'. He flips a switch and it flickers on real bright. There's a cot in the middle of the room. Somethin' covered in a sheet is lyin' on it.

Dr. Comeaux is right. The air smells worse than that cow Chickie stabbed.

He puts his handkerchief over his nose and mouth and goes over to the body. He pulls back the sheet.

I walk up closer. It's an animal really. Nothin' particular human about it. It's all blowed up and purple and gray and black.

He waves me closer.

He says take a good look, son. Is this your father?

I put the handkerchief over my nose and take one more step toward the cot and look hard. There ain't much face, true, but the hair could be Daddy's. It's parted about the same way. The remainin' eye is dark, like Daddy's. The chin is kinda like Daddy's too.

I notice the jagged gray stump of the chewed-off leg.

This thing could be Daddy, but still I'm not sure.

I tell Dr. Comeaux well, I dunno. Maybe.

He says well, son, I know this is hard but I need to ask you to keep tryin'.

I stare again, feelin' sicker.

He says do you want me to flip him over? Maybe from the back you could . . .

His voice trails off.

I say, well, I guess so.

Dr. Comeaux walks to a nearby metal desk and opens a drawer. He gits out some rubber gloves and puts them on. He comes back, grabs the body quick by one arm and the leg that's left, and turns it over.

I gasp. On the right shoulder, there's a

tattoo of a snake coiled around a rose. The snake is blue, the rose is red. I feel a little faint.

I hear myself sayin' oh my God. I hobble fast as I can from the room, chokin' back sobs. I barely make it out of the door when I vomit hard into the handkerchief.

Captain Landry runs after me and so does Dr. Comeaux. By the time we all git out the door I've got tears runnin' down my face. I hear myself sobbin' oh Daddy, oh Daddy. It don't even seem like my own voice.

Captain Landry says I'm awfully sorry, Meely.

Dr. Comeaux says me too, son. We'll make sure he gets a decent burial.

They don't ax me outright so I guess I haven't actually lied.

But it ain't Daddy. Daddy ain't never had a tattoo in his life. Daddy spoke against such things.

Daddy's alive out there. Somewhere.

28

A whole load of people show up for Daddy's funeral, a lot more than I figgered would. Seems to me about half of Catahoula Bayou is here. Funny how some people ain't never got nothin' much good to say about you when you were alive but come to wish you well now that you're dead. This is another thing Daddy would call hypocritical.

Captain Landry's made it so I could git out of jail for the services. Sergeant Picou wanted cuffs on me but Captain Landry said no. Anyway, how could I run with this busted leg?

I'm done cryin' over the fact that it ain't Daddy. I even think it's possible I'll see him again. So I just stare away and look serious. Everybody thinks I'm bein' brave.

Daddy would git a hoot out of this, too.

They're buryin' Daddy in a little cement tomb way at the back of the Catholic cemetery just inside the fence from the cane field. Momma's buried here too in a bigger tomb up front that her family paid for when she died. Daddy says that's about the only thing her family ever done for Momma after she got married.

I've always liked the cemetery. All those whitewashed tombs set in rows with their crosses. Rich people like the Heberts have big marble tombs all speckled and shiny with angels and such on top of 'em. They keep the grass cut and plant flowers in the spring and summer. I come here now and then to visit Momma's grave, though it's true I haven't come much lately. Miz Lirette explained to me that they tried to git the plot next to Momma but it was too much money and this plot is the best they can do for now. I think it's better, really — seein' how it ain't Daddy.

I feel pretty bad about this poor man in the coffin. I wonder about his kin and whether they're worried about him. I wonder if he could be a hobo from someplace. Daddy says he sometimes meets hobos up at Yankee City where they come down from the North to do oil field work. Most of them are nice fellas just a bit down on their luck, he says.

It's a hot day and I'm dressed in a suit and tie that Miz Lirette's bought for me at the Bargain Store in town. I'm sweatin' like a pig in a slaughter line but Miz Lirette says I look mighty handsome dressed up and Momma and Daddy would be proud. Momma prob'ly would.

Daddy would git a big belly laugh at me spruced up like a Fuller Brush salesman. Daddy never owned but one suit and that's the one he married Momma in. Then he refused to ever wear it again.

I kinda like this suit myself as I've never wore one before. I looked in the mirror once after I put it on and hardly recognized myself. This tie, though, is about to strangle me.

At the cemetery Captain Landry and Miz Lirette stand at my side and a whole bunch of people stand behind us. I notice Joey Hebert and his daddy and momma and Chickie and his momma and a slew of other people from Catahoula Bayou. One of them is Mary Portier, who sits improper. Another is Claudia Toups, my cousin who never talks to me.

Daddy would get a hoot out of this, too.

Way in the back, behind everybody else, I see Cassie and Miz Jackson.

I see the sister who I met at the hospital. She comes up out of the pack and cups my chin and says God be with you, Emile. I'm so sorry about this.

The long black hearse drives up and they

take the coffin out. It's not a bad coffin — it's made of pine, what I know about wood. Father Giroir, the priest for Catahoula, comes up and sprinkles holy water on it and says some things.

He says Logan LaBauve was a troubled soul and he fought all of his life against the demons of liquor and loneliness. But we do know that in his life he loved his dear departed wife, Elizabeth, a good and decent woman, and he loved his son, Emile. We pray that he found God before he died and that he is now with God in heaven.

He then closes his eyes and crosses hisself and says a silent prayer.

I would have added that Daddy was the best gator hunter and tracker in the whole world but I guess that's not somethin' people say at funerals.

When Father's finished the undertaker comes over and hands me a small bunch of flowers and says here, son, put these on your daddy's coffin after we lower it in the tomb.

I do so and close my eyes and say to myself I hope this poor man, whoever he is, has gone someplace good.

Afterward, Miz Lirette says it's proper that I should stand in line and receive folks. So I do. I shake a lot of hands, some of 'em of people I don't even know. Joey comes by and says sorry, Meely, your daddy was a real character and Mr. Hebert even says it's a shame, son, and I'm really sorry. Miz Breaux hugs me, as does Mary Portier. She smells sweet and for some reason my heart does a little pitty-patter when I look into her eyes, which are blue and clear. She says this is all too sad, Meely, for a boy not to have anybody and pulls me closer.

And when I look at her again I can see she has tears in her eyes and I realize I have a feelin' for Mary that I don't think I had before, though I cain't say exactly what it is.

Finally Cassie and Miz Jackson come and Miz Jackson says we knew your daddy as a good man and we'll miss him. He always did right by us and he felt for the people who didn't have much. You cain't say that about everybody in this world, Meely.

Cassie is behind her and comes up and leans forward. She smells like store-bought soap and looks all growed up in her store-bought dress and silk ribbons in her hair.

I decide Cassie is not just pretty but beautiful and my heart goes racy again.

She leans close and whispers oh, Meely, I'm sorry 'bout your daddy. He was a good man and he always treated us with respect and we'll always remember him in a nice way, don't matter what the law says about him. And I hope you're all right. And don't you never tell nobody but I've got a secret.

She pulls me real close and whispers Chilly's alive. He's okay.

29

Mr. Dorsey comes to see me in jail the day after the funeral and says Emile, we're going to court. I believe we will be able to show the judge that Junior and his uncle are lying. Besides, with your daddy being dead and their not having found Chilly, they can't keep saying they have to keep you locked up as a witness. So I've applied for a hearing before Judge Pettibone. He's an honest man. It's set for ten in the morning.

I say that's okay with me, Mr. Dorsey. I'm gittin' a bit tired of jail and I wouldn't mind goin' fishin' and such.

He says the other thing is that since both of your parents are dead the state's already moved to put you in an orphanage should you be let off. But we think we've got a better idea.

I say Mr. Dorsey, I cain't see goin' to any orphanage so I'm interested in whatever it is you've thought of.

He says all right, we'll talk about that later, Emile. The thing about this hearing is that the prosecutor will ask you all kinds of hard questions and might accuse you of this or that or say bad things about your daddy. Junior and his uncle will be there, too, and they might be called as witnesses to say things against you. There could be folks you know and lots you don't, including some policemen. You just have to be ready for this and not get flustered.

I say I'll try not to.

He says what we're trying to do is show the judge that not only are all those things that Junior and his uncle have said about you untrue, but that Junior has provoked you at every chance.

Provoked?

Emile, that means he picked on you and badgered you and bullied you till you got tired of it and hit back.

I say Mr. Dorsey, that about covers it as far as I'm concerned.

He says now, Emile, we've got a few people lined up on our side.

Like who?

Well Miz Lirette for one. And Cassie Jackson. And Mrs. Jackson, if we need her to talk about your condition after the beating by Junior and his friends.

I say what about Joey Hebert? He saw Junior throw the bat.

Mr. Dorsey says well, I've talked to Joey

and he doesn't want to get involved. He says lots of kids saw Junior throw the bat and I should talk to them.

This stumps me a bit.

Mr. Dorsey continues. Honestly, Emile, if there weren't others we could get to testify about these matters we could get the judge to issue something called a subpoena. That's an order from the court that would make Joey come and tell what he'd seen, even if he doesn't want to. But since he is a friend of yours, I wasn't sure that would be best.

I puzzle over this a moment. I say, well, there *were* lots of others.

Mr. Dorsey says we've found one in particular who saw the fight and heard things afterward that were a lot more interesting.

Who?

Charles Naquin.

I say I've never heard of Charles Naquin.

He says I think you call him Chickie.

I say Chickie? Chickie's comin' to court?

He is indeed, Emile. Charles told Miss Lirette he'd heard things from some of Junior's bunch that might help us a great deal. He's willing to say them to the judge.

I say Chickie has? Well, good ole Chickie. Only thing is, Mr. Dorsey, I shore hope Chickie washes first.

Washes?

I say yes sir. Chickie never washes or at least if he does he don't use good soap.

He says is that right?

I say yes sir, that's right. It don't matter to me so much but it does make Chickie unpopular at school. 'Specially with Junior and that bunch.

Mr. Dorsey cups his chin in his hand and says hhm. Well, Emile, maybe I'll have Miss Lirette call Chickie's parents to make sure he washes before tomorrow.

I say that's prob'ly a good idea. But Chickie's only really got a momma. His daddy's a vegetable, people say.

He says a vegetable?

Yes sir. He had some stroke or such and just lays there.

Mr. Dorsey nods and says okay, Emile, is there anything else I should know about Charles?

I say let me think. Uh, he's got pimples all over his face and his shirt never stays tucked in and he's what some people call fat. That's about it. Oh, and he likes to talk. Junior sometimes calls him Motor Mouth.

Mr. Dorsey nods again and says those are good things to know. You get a good night's sleep and I'll see you in the morning. By the way, Emile, wear that suit again, if you don't mind.

I say Mr. Dorsey life is curious. I've not worn a suit ever and now I'm wearin' one every day.

He says well, son, you now know what it feels like to be a lawyer.

I say I guess I do. How is it that you stand them stiff collars and them strangly ties?

He says you know, you just get used to them, Meely.

I realize this is the first time Mr. Dorsey has called me Meely.

I say yes sir, I guess it's true that you can git used to almost anything.

Mr. Dorsey nods his head. He gits up and leaves.

I realize how lonesome the jail has become and how I miss our house, saggy and tired as it is. I can understand now why Daddy give up on jail.

Us LaBauves need to be out under the sky, where the rabbits and the coons and the gators are. We just need to go fishin' sometimes.

I shore hope Mr. Dorsey is as smart as I think he is.

I wouldn't make it in reform school. I just wouldn't.

30

When me and Mr. Dorsey git to court, it's
quiet as a sleepin' cat. We've come early so
Mr. Dorsey can show me where we'll sit
and where I'll have to go up and tell the
truth to the judge. We sit at our own table,
facin' where the judge sits.

Pretty soon people start to come in.
There's a big man with wavy red hair. Mr.
Dorsey says he's Mr. Aucoin, the prosecutor. He sits at his own table at the left of
ours. He says hello, Alphonse, but he don't
look at me. He acts like I might be invisible
or somethin', which I cain't say I like.

There's a blond woman, young with
thick glasses but kinda pretty. Mr. Dorsey
says she's the court reporter.

There's another man with glasses, a crew
cut, and a gray suit. Mr. Dorsey says he's
the bailiff.

Then some police come in, includin'
Captain Landry and Sergeant Picou and
Uncle and a few more, all in uniforms.
They don't look happy.

There's no sight of Junior yet, which in a

way I'm glad for. It's bad enough havin' to be in the same room with ugly ole Uncle.

Then I see Miz Lirette and Miz Breaux and Joey Hebert and Claudia Toups. They come in and all sit together. I knew Miz Lirette would be here 'cause she's gonna testify for me. But I'm surprised to see Joey and Claudia. Then Mr. Hebert himself trails in and sits in the row behind 'em.

Then Cassie and Miz Jackson come in and sit in the very back row.

Then Junior comes in. He's got a suit on, too. He don't look at me.

Somehow I think it's funny that me and Junior both have got stuck in suits, even though we're against each other. I'll bet Junior hates his tie as much as I hate mine.

Finally Chickie comes in. I hardly recognize Chickie. He don't have on a suit but he's wearin' what looks like close to church clothes. Black pants and a white shirt and a wide blue 'n' white tie that comes down about to where his belly button would be. He's got his hair slicked back and it's so shiny I figger he's put Brylcreem in it.

Or knowin' Chickie, prob'ly lard.

After a while longer, the judge comes in. He's short and mostly bald with gray where he has hair. He don't look mean but he looks serious as a crow in winter, which

237

I guess a judge has to be.

A man says all rise for the Honorable Judge Ashley Pettibone.

We all stand up till the judge sits down. Then we do, too.

The judge says I'm going to ask everybody who's been called as a witness to go out into the hall and wait until you're called to the stand. After your testimony is over, I will ask you to return to the hall. Thank you.

The room about half empties out. Miz Jackson goes with Cassie. Three policemen, none that I know, stay behind, as do Miz Breaux, Joey and Claudia Toups and Mr. Hebert.

The judge says Mr. Dorsey, you called for this hearing. You may proceed.

Mr. Dorsey gits up and straightens his tie and looks at the judge and says I've filed a motion before the court for the immediate release of Emile LaBauve. I believe we have evidence that will prove the state has no reason to hold him in jail one minute longer.

The judge says Mr. Aucoin?

We object, Your Honor. The charges against Emile LaBauve are serious and if he's let out of jail he'll likely run away, as did his father. The state has many witnesses who will show the state has more than good evidence to charge him with the crimes laid out at the arraignment.

The judge says well, gentlemen, let's proceed.

Then Mr. Dorsey says, I call Emile LaBauve.

I go up to the place where I'm to sit and the bailiff holds out a Bible and says do you swear that you will tell the truth so help you God?

I say I do.

Mr. Dorsey then axes me to start from the beginnin' about me and Junior. I tell pretty much the whole story again, changin' the part about callin' Junior a possum's ass to a possum's butt, since I don't think it's polite to say ass before the judge. I git to the day Junior and Uncle was waitin' for me and how they had Chilly hogtied and how Daddy come git us all loose and how we drove off in the truck, and the wreck and such. I tell why Daddy slipped away 'cause he felt the law was against him and why I stayed to tell our side.

Mr. Dorsey says no further questions.

Then the prosecutor gits up and says Emile, what kind of relationship did you have with your father?

Well me and Daddy got along okay.
Did your father ever hit you?
No sir.
Never?
Never.
Did your father ever drink liquor?
Yes sir.
You ever see your father drunk?
Yes sir, I did a few times.
Is it true your father was often absent and left you alone?
Well, Daddy's a gator hunter and as I no longer have a momma, I did tend to stay by myself.
Is it true that during this time you were often truant from school?
What's truant?
You didn't go.
I went some but not always.
And is it true your father encouraged you to stay away from school?
I don't like this question much 'cause I know what he's gittin' at.
I say well, Daddy said school never did much for him. So he left it up to me.
I see. So your father basically left you to do as you pleased?
I s'pose he did. After Momma died it is true Daddy give up on a lot of things. But he never give up on me.

The prosecutor stops a moment and wipes his brow with a handkerchief he fetches from his coat pocket. He says the day of the altercation with Joseph Guidry on the softball field, is it true that you teased him and called him names?

Sorry, but what's an altercation? And by Joseph Guidry do you mean Junior?

An altercation is a squabble and, yes, Joseph is the boy you know as Junior.

I realize I never knowed Junior's real name.

I say I guess I did call Junior a possum name but only after Junior axed me about whether Daddy was in prison yet and called me trash, which I'm not, and then said I was a sabine, which for Junior is the same as callin' somebody that other ignorant word.

What ignorant word?

It's not a word I like to say. Momma and Daddy both told me it was a mean, ignorant word and I ought not to say it.

The judge says you can say it, Emile.

Nigger. Sabine for Junior is the same as nigger.

The prosecutor says well, Emile, did anybody else hear Joseph say this?

Shore, Junior's whole gang, Roddy and that bunch was all standin' right there.

But nobody else?

No sir, nobody was there yet at the soft-ball field but Junior's gang.

So we'll just have to take your word for that, is that what you're saying?

Yes sir. I guess that's right.

The prosecutor pauses for a minute to look at a yellow notepad in his hand.

Now moving forward to the day you were brought to jail, do you remember that day, Emile?

I say Mr. Aucoin, that's kind of a hard day to forgit.

He says is it true that on that day you and one Chester Cox lay in wait to ambush Joseph Guidry as he walked past your house?

Is Chester the same as Chilly?

That's right.

Then no sir, we did no such thing.

And is it true, after you ambushed Joseph Guidry, that his uncle, Sergeant Joseph Guidry, happened to be driving by and saw you and tried to intervene?

I realize I never knowed Junior was named the same as Uncle. I say no sir, that's not what happened at all.

And when he did, is it true that your father stepped out of the cane field with his double-barrel Winchester shotgun and disarmed Officer Guidry?

Well, Daddy stepped out of the cane field with his gun but that was only 'cause —

And after you and your father and Chester Cox tied up and beat Officer Guidry and Joseph, is it true you then tortured them by putting fire ants down their pants?

Mr. Dorsey rises and says object, Your Honor. Emile here already says he didn't tie up or beat either one of them.

The judge says Mr. Aucoin, ask the question differently.

Emile, did you and Chester Cox put red ants on Joseph and Officer Guidry?

No sir, I didn't but Chilly did that but only after he'd been beat and stuck with a lit cigarette and after Uncle had busted me on the head with his gun and we were all tied up together and Junior had called Momma names and such. Like I said before.

Mr. Aucoin looks at me good for the first time.

I say maybe Chilly shouldn't have done that but I s'pect Chilly was mad, as I was, too.

So Emile, you have a bad temper do you?

Mr. Dorsey stands up and objects again.

The judge says Emile you can answer the question.

I say well, when it comes to Junior I guess I do.

And you were dying to get back at Junior because you felt he sometimes picked on you at school, weren't you? You wanted revenge on Junior, didn't you?

Mr. Dorsey objects again. Your honor, Mr. Aucoin is badgering this boy.

The judge fiddles with his glasses and says Mr. Aucoin, really. I think that's enough speechifyin'. But I would like Emile to answer the question.

He looks at me. Truthfully, Emile.

Yes sir. Well, if you're axin' whether I liked beatin' on Junior with that stick, I'd say I did after what he done to me. But I've always tried to ignore Junior just like Miz Lirette told me to do. But Junior ain't so easy to ignore. Junior gits on a lot of people, and not just me. Go ax anybody.

Mr. Aucoin fiddles with his tie. He says so you admit you dislike Junior?

Yes sir. But you wouldn't like him much either if he was beatin' on you.

The prosecutor looks at me and shakes his head and says no other questions, Your Honor.

The judge tells me I can go sit back with Mr. Dorsey, who then calls Miz Lirette. She comes in and puts her hand on the Bible and swears.

Mr. Dorsey says please, ma'am, how long have you known Emile LaBauve?

I guess all his life. I was somewhat friendly with his mother before she died. We knew each other from church. And I teach Emile in ninth grade.

What kind of student is he?

Emile is a good student when he applies himself.

Would you say he's bright?

Very bright.

Does he often miss school?

Yes, unfortunately he does.

Is Emile a problem when he's at school?

No, Emile's never given us a problem.

But he has been to the principal's office several times, is that right?

Well, Mrs. Breaux, our principal, is always trying to get Emlie to come to school regularly. So she sometimes does call Emile into the office to talk to him, that's true.

Does Emile have a history of picking on Joseph Guidry?

No, the opposite. I don't like to characterize any of our students as bad children.

But Joseph Guidry has a history of bullying other students.

Did he ever bully Emile?

On two occasions I witnessed Joseph calling Emile names. And once on the softball field before this last incident he was ready to attack Emile and I intervened. And Joseph has been in Mrs. Breaux's office several times for picking fights with other students.

On the day that Joseph and Emile were running in the schoolhouse, who was chasing who?

Joseph was after Emile.

Did he appear angry?

Very. It was quite unsettling.

And would you describe what happened as they ran down the hall?

I walked out of my classroom after I heard the first footsteps. I saw Joseph going after Emile. Then Joseph crashed into Mrs. Breaux.

And what did Emile do then?

Nothing. After Mrs. Breaux recovered herself, she ordered both Joseph and Emile into the office.

Did Emile object?

No, he went without objection.

Did he say anything then or there that would have upset Joseph?

No, he didn't say a word to Joseph.

Mr. Dorsey says thank you, no more questions.

The prosecutor rises and adjusts his suit coat and says isn't it true, Miss Lirette, that students who are truant are generally turned over to the proper authorities?

That is sometimes the case, but it depends a lot on circumstances.

But in the case of Emlie that isn't true?

No, it's not. Mrs. Breaux feels, and I do too, that Emile needs to be encouraged, not punished.

So you've made an exception for Emile. He's treated like a special case?

Well, given his family circumstances, we thought allowing him to stay in school would be best.

So you're aware that Emile spends long periods of time without supervision.

Unfortunately, yes.

The day of the last altercation on the softball field, you didn't actually see it, did you?

No, not until Emile and Joseph came running into the hall.

And when you were at the field earlier, you didn't notice a squabble between Joseph and Emile, did you?

No, I didn't.

You spoke to Joseph?

Yes.

What did he say?

Good morning, as I recall.

He was polite?

Yes, and so was Emile.

The times you described earlier that you heard Joseph calling Emile names, he didn't actually attack Emile, did he?

No. But once he intended to. I intervened.

And what sort of names was Joseph calling Emile?

I don't really remember.

Common schoolyard taunts?

I guess you could say that, though Emile said Junior said very ugly things to him — called him a sabine and trash.

But you didn't hear those things yourself?

No, I didn't.

And you are aware that Emile sometimes did name-calling of his own?

I'm aware that Junior said so.

But the day of the altercation in Mrs. Breaux's office, Emile confessed to having called Junior names, didn't he?

He did.

Thank you, Miss Lirette. I have no more questions.

Then Mr. Dorsey calls Cassie Jackson. She comes through the swingin' wooden door of the court wearin' her Sunday clothes and she walks like somebody who knows what she's doin' and she puts her hand on the Bible and swears in a clear voice.

Mr. Dorsey says Cassie, you live down Catahoula Bayou, don't you?

Yes sir.

Not too far from the LaBauve house?

A mile and a half, I'd say.

Did you witness the trouble between Emile and Junior Guidry that day in the cornfield?

Yes sir.

And what did you see?

I was comin' to look for Meely, who I thought might have a mess of fish. He'd given us some the day before. Anyway, I hear this commotion out on the edge of the field and cain't imagine what it is. Then I see the one called Junior has a big stick and he's beatin' Meely hard. There are maybe five or six other boys and they're hittin' on him, too. One of them had put a sack over Meely's head.

Then what happened?

I yelled at 'em to stop. What they was doin' was terrible.

And then?

249

Junior says to me all huffed up who the hell are you? Then Chilly — Chilly Cox who was with me — says to Junior who the hell are you?

Now, Chilly is the same as Chester Cox, is that right?

Yes sir.

He's a friend of yours?

Yes sir. We're at school together. He lives five or six miles from us up the bayou.

And why did Chilly happen to be there that day?

He'd come over to our house to visit. I wasn't there but Momma told Chilly I might be over near the place where Meely fishes since I'd got some fish from him the day before.

So Chilly caught up with you, right?

Yes sir.

Then what happened?

Well, like I said Chilly walked out and said to Junior who the hell are you and then Junior told Chilly you stay out of this, nigger.

In just those words?

Yes sir. Just those words.

And then?

Well, Chilly didn't know or care nothin' about this Junior character one way or another but he shore didn't like that, so he ran over to Junior and pulled him up by the collar. Chilly's big, you see. Real big. He's nineteen, older than most of the kids at school. But he's big, even for nineteen.

Has Chilly had trouble with school? Is that why he's older than most of the other students?

No sir. Chilly's plenty smart. But he had to quit school now and then to go to work 'cause his family's poor. So are most colored folk down Catahoula Bayou.

Cassie, getting back to the altercation, did Chilly hit Junior?

No sir. He threw him down on the ground and then told him to bend over so Meely could hit him with the stick he'd been hittin' Meely with.

And did Junior do so?

Yes sir. Junior seemed scared. He wasn't huffin' no more. He bent over and Meely hit him three or four times on the backsides.

And then?

Meely axed Chilly if he'd hold them other boys so he could whack 'em too.

And what did they do then?

They all run off. Junior with 'em. Like chickens from a barkin' dog.

Thank you, Cassie. Your Honor, I have

251

no other questions.

Mr. Aucoin says Cassie, did you know Emile's father?

Yes sir, some.

Did he come around your house ever?

Yes sir, sellin' coons and such to Momma and other folks.

You liked Emile's father?

Yes sir, everybody did. He was a character.

And did you know that Mr. LaBauve was now and then in trouble with the law?

Yes sir, everybody knew that, too. His wife had passed some time before and folks said he took it hard at first. Some folks say he still does.

And you and Emile are good friends, is that right?

I guess you could say that.

You've known each other a long time?

Well, it turns out Momma says we've knowed each other since we were babies. But we hadn't spoke for a long time till recently.

And what is it you and Emlie talk about?

Cassie looks surprised at this question. For the first time she looks at me. Curious too.

She says, uh, well, all kinds of things.

For instance?

Fishin'. Meely, him, he's some fisherman.

Anything else?

Gators. Meely hunts gators, too, like his daddy. And snakes, too.

What else?

You mean what else he hunts or what else we talk about?

Talk about.

Cassie seems flustered for the first time.

Uh, well, uh, lemme see, uh, uh, religion.

Religion?

Yes sir. I'm religious, you know. Me and Momma go to Mandalay Baptist. It's a little country church. Meely's kinda religious, too. You know my daddy passed away some time ago and poor Meely's lost his momma and now his daddy. So sometimes we talk about things like God. Like God and, uh, heaven.

Cassie looks at the prosecutor real serious.

She says Meely's real fond of talkin' about heaven.

I put my head down on my table. I cain't look at Cassie anymore.

Heaven? So Emile has his mind on heaven, does he?

Yes sir, pretty much all the time I'd say.

The prosecutor fiddles with his bow tie again. He says so the point is, you and Emile talk about everything. You consider him a very close friend, yes?

Yes sir, I guess he is.

He gave you a mess of fish for your family, is that right?

Yes sir. Good fish, too. They fried up real nice.

I see. Well, Cassie, people sometimes lie for their friends, don't they?

Mr. Dorsey says object. The judge says Mr. Aucoin, ask the question differently.

The prosecutor says Cassie, you would have no reason to lie for Emile, would you?

No sir.

And what about Chilly Cox?

What about him?

He was your boyfriend, right?

Cassie looks at me again. She says he was. But we had broke up.

But you still liked him, didn't you?

Yes sir.

And when you tell us Emile here is innocent, you're also telling us your boyfriend is innocent, too. Is that right?

Mr. Dorsey says object.

Cassie answers anyway. She says well he *is* innocent. It happened just like I said.

But Chester ran away, didn't he? He ran away instead of staying and trying to straighten things out.

Yes sir, I guess he did.

And why would an innocent boy run?

Mr. Dorsey says object, he's asking for an opinion not to mention badgering the witness.

The judge says Mr. Dorsey's right, Mr. Aucoin. But I'll let Cassie answer.

Cassie don't say nothin' for a minute. Then she says well, if them policemen had already beat you once, you'da prob'ly run, too. I would've. It's different if you're colored. Some police think all us colored folk are guilty of *somethin'*.

The prosecutor looks at Cassie and shakes his head and then looks down at his pad and says no other questions.

The judge calls for a small break and we stretch our legs and I drink a glass of water. Then Mr. Dorsey stands back up and says I call Charles Naquin.

Chickie comes in. He walks down the aisle, tuckin' his white shirt into his britches. His tie has somehow gotten shorter than it was. So has his britches. He gits up on the stand and mops the sweat off his face with his shirtsleeve and says the words on the Bible.

Mr. Dorsey says do you know Emile LaBauve?

Yes sir, he's at my school.

Are you friends?

Yes sir, I think we are.

He looks at me and I nod.

He says yes sir, we are. Since I started school.

How long ago was that?

I'm in eighth grade now.

Were you present on the day when Joseph Guidry attacked Emile with a baseball bat?

The prosecutor says objection. Now Mr. Dorsey is editorializing.

The judge says Mr. Aucoin, I'll figure out whether it was or was not an attack. Let him answer.

He says yes sir.

Mr. Dorsey says do you know what happened that sparked that incident?

I didn't see the very first thing, when Junior called Meely trash and those things but I —

Mr. Aucoin stands up and says object, Your Honor. This boy is testifying to hearsay.

Mr. Dorsey says Judge, I'll ask it a different way. Charles, tell us what you actually saw, not what you heard.

Chickie says I was standin' by the back-stop. I don't play ball. I hate to run 'cause I've got weak lungs, Momma says. I played right field once and a fly ball hit me right on top of the head. I was in bed two days. Momma thought I had a concussion. I was in a bad way. Terrible headaches you wouldn't believe.

Mr. Dorsey interrupts and says Charles, I understand that. But please, get to the question.

Yes sir. Well, I was standin' by the back-stop and Meely was just goin' out on the field when one of Junior's henchmen — uh, I think it was —

Mr. Aucoin stands up again and says Your Honor, please instruct this witness to keep his opinions to himself.

The judge looks stern at Chickie. He says young man, whether Junior Guidry's friends are henchmen is something this court will decide. Now just answer the question.

Chickie says yes sir. Like I said, Meely was takin' the field and next thing I know one of Junior's friends is sayin' kinda loud Junior's gonna whip that little LaBauve's ass good one day and then Meely slides by Junior and Junior looks at Meely ugly and Meely says some words to him and I thought Junior was gonna explode. That boy's got a terrible temper.

Mr. Aucoin jumps up again. Object, Your Honor!

Mr. Dorsey raises his hand before the judge can say anything and says Charles, again we don't want your opinion of Junior. We simply want to know what you saw.

Chickie says okay, Meely's team started chantin' strike out, Junior, strike out. And he did. That cracked me up.

Mr. Dorsey says and after the strikeout?

Oh, it was horrible. Junior tried to kill Meely with that big black bat of his. He's like Frankenstein I'm tellin' you. Out of control, I mean crazy. Cra-zy. He was goin' for Meely's head and —

The prosecutor says objection, Judge, this boy is not testifying, he's smearing the reputation of a young man who's not even on trial!

Chickie says well, he should be on trial!

The judge raps his gavel hard and says Charles, I've told you for the last time stick to what happened. Do you understand me?

Chickie nods. Okay. Uh, I mean, yes sir.

The judge says go on, Mr. Dorsey.

Charles, just describe what happened with the bat.

Junior threw it at Meely. Real hard. Hard enough to kill — uh, I mean real hard. Meely jumped up and the bat barely missed him. The bat rolled all the way into center field.

Then what?

Meely ran into the schoolhouse with Junior right behind.

And you didn't see anything after that, is that right?

No sir, but I heard that Junior was about to kill Miz Breaux and a few other teachers and —

The prosecutor stands up to object again but Mr. Dorsey says excuse me, Charles, but since others were there and have already told us what happened, I won't have to ask you that.

Chickie looks disappointed. He says, oh, okay.

Mr. Dorsey says now, Charles, were you at school the day after the incident?

Yes sir.

Was Emile there?

No sir.

And did you hear anything that would shed light on later events?

Yes sir. I was in the boys' room with Junior and two of his henchmen.

Mr. Aucoin shouts objection!

259

The judge shakes his finger at Chickie. He says Charles, do you want to join Emile in juvenile lockup tonight?

No sir.

Well, son, I think there's plenty of room for you there and you will be sent there if you keep this up. Do you understand me?

Chickie looks down again and says sorry, Your Honor.

The judge says now, Charles, just tell what happened like it happened. You don't need to say more than that.

Okay. I was in the boys' room with Junior and Roddy Bergeron and Jerome Giroir. They were talkin' about Meely.

And who are Roddy and Jerome?

Podnahs of Junior's. They hang around together.

Chickie looks at the judge. Is that okay?

The judge says that's fine, Charles. That's fine.

Mr. Dorsey says and why were you there?

I was smokin' cigarettes.

With Junior and his friends?

No sir. *Because* of Junior and his friends.

I don't understand.

They make me smoke. They want to see how many I can smoke at one time.

Make you smoke?

260

Yes sir. Force me.

Hhm, I see. And Charles, how do they make you smoke?

They threaten to —

Chickie stops and looks up at the judge. He says can I tell this part, Your Honor?

Charles, you can as long as what you say is what you personally know to be true and not just what you've heard from other people.

Okay. Well they threatened to whip my butt if I don't. Throw me in the bayou. Pull down my pants at recess. Oh, and torture me too. Torture me with brandin' irons.

Okay, Charles, let me see if I understand this. So you're in the boys' room and Joseph and his friends are making you smoke?

That's right. I had three cigarettes in my mouth and one up my nose.

Up your nose?

Yes sir. It's actually not so bad havin' one up your nose. Two gits pretty rough. 'Specially 'cause of my weak lungs.

I see. Then what happened?

Well, see, after I had one up my nose and three in my mouth I started coughin' real bad and they were bored with me anyway so they started talkin'.

And what were they talking about?

They were talkin' about how they had ambushed Emile after school.

Ambushed?

Yes sir. Junior or Joseph — which should I call him?

Either one.

Okay. Junior was real mad 'cause they'd all gone to ambush Emile and had caught him on the edge of Cancienne's cornfield and were givin' him a good — a good, uh — Mr. Dorsey, should I say just what they said? It ain't very nice.

Yes you should, Charles. The judge will understand that this isn't the way you talk.

Junior said they were givin' him a good ass kickin' like that little sabine deserved when some nigger girl and a giant nigger boy stepped out of the field.

Did they say what happened then?

Junior said if he didn't have such, uh — should I say it, Mr. Dorsey?

You can say it, Charles.

Junior said if he didn't have such chicken-shit friends, we could've whipped that big ole nigger, too.

Then what happened?

Junior cussed Roddy and Jerome and he punched the wall and left the boys' room.

And then?

Well, after Junior left, Jerome said Junior was just mad 'cause he's the one who really chickened out. He said Junior coulda fought the giant but he was too scared. Then Roddy said yeah that's right. He said first of all if Junior had fought the nigger we'd've all piled on. But he didn't. Roddy said it served Junior right that Meely whacked him with that stick.

Did they say anything else?

They said Junior was uh, was . . .

Go ahead, Charles.

Jerome said anyway they were glad they weren't Meely 'cause Junior was real pissed off and he was gonna git his uncle from the police in town and they was gonna find that nigger and kick his ass. He said then they were gonna catch Meely and finish the job they had started.

You're sure about this, Charles?

Scout's honor.

Chickie raises three fingers of his right hand.

After you left the boys' room what happened?

Nothin' much. Roddy told me I better not say anything or I'd end up like Meely.

But you decided to say something?

Yes sir. They think I'm chicken but I'm not. Not really. Not always.

Mr. Dorsey says thank you, Charles. No more questions.

The prosecutor rises and looks serious at Chickie. He says Charles, we knew you were coming here today and we knew what you were going to say. I assume you are aware of that?

I guess so.

And we've done a little checking of our own, so you won't mind if I ask you some questions about what you just said, will you?

No sir.

And you do remember that you've taken an oath on the Bible?

Yes sir.

And do you know what perjury is?

No sir.

Well perjury is when you lie under oath. You are aware that perjury itself is a crime? You could go to jail for perjury.

Mr. Dorsey says objection. He's trying to intimidate the witness.

The judge says move on, Mr. Aucoin.

The prosecutor says Charles, do you ever smoke when you're not being forced to by Joseph and his friends?

Chickie looks at the judge. He says do I have to answer, Your Honor?

The judge says yes, you have to.

Yeah. I mean, yes sir.

Does your mother know you smoke?

No sir, she doesn't.

Would she approve?

No sir.

So you go around sneaking cigarettes, is that right?

Mr. Dorsey says object, Your Honor. What's the point?

The judge says I'll let Mr. Aucoin go on but please get to the point.

Chickie says I guess I do.

And the day you were allegedly being bullied in the boys' room by Junior and his friends, whose cigarettes were you smoking?

Uh, my own.

Your own?

Yes sir, Chesterfields.

And didn't you once go around bragging at school how you could smoke three or four or even five cigarettes at one time?

Uh, well, I don't really remember.

Well, Charles, let me help you remember. I think once you might have said this in front of Miss Lirette when you didn't realize she was standing near you, is that right?

Uh, it might be.

And you got sent to the principal's office, right?

Uh, well, I don't know, uh —

And Mrs. Breaux, your principal, took

your cigarettes away and paddled your britches, is that right?

Uh, well, uh, I don't —

Charles, please. As you know, Miss Lirette's here, as is Mrs. Breaux. We can put them up here on the stand and ask them, if you'd like.

Uh, no sir. I guess that's right.

You guess?

No sir, that's right.

Charles, are you popular at school?

Mr. Dorsey says Your Honor, what kind of question is that?

The judge says what kind of question *is* that, Mr. Aucoin?

It's leading to a point, Your Honor.

Well, it better be. Okay, I'll let it go. You can answer, Charles.

No. I guess I'm not popular.

People tease you?

Junior and his gang — uh, I mean friends — do.

Any others?

Some others.

Almost everybody would you say?

Not Meely.

Ah, I see. Meely doesn't tease you. You're best friends, is that right?

Kinda.

Kinda?

Meely and me talk a lot. We do stuff now and then. We went crawfishin' together once.

The prosecutor says okay. Now, on that day in the boys' room, what happened before you went in there?

Uh, I dunno what you mean, uh —

Didn't you go up to Roddy Bergeron and ask if he'd like to see a trick?

Uh, I don't remember if —

And didn't Roddy say go away, Chickie, you're bothering me?

No.

No? Are you sure, Charles?

Yes.

Then Charles, what *did* he say?

He said go away fatso, you stink.

Hhm, I see. And what did you say back?

I said I can smoke four cigarettes at once, includin' one up my nose.

And did you volunteer to show this trick to Roddy?

Uh, I guess I might've.

And what did Roddy say then?

He said okay, fat ass, I gotta see this. Wait here while I git Junior.

And Junior came?

With Jerome, that's right.

So you went voluntarily into the boys' room with Joseph and Roddy and

267

Jerome, is that right?

I guess so.

You guess so?

I did.

And no one threatened to beat you up to make you smoke those cigarettes, did they?

Uh, well, Junior said this better be good, fatso, or that's your ass.

But he didn't threaten you to make you smoke, right?

Chickie looks down for a long time. Finally he says well, no, but I know that Junior and if —

So you lied about that, didn't you, Charles?

Chickie stammers and says well, no, not about that other stuff with Meely. I —

The prosecutor cuts him off. He says I think we've heard enough about that.

By this time poor Chickie is in a state. His face is cayenne red and he's sweatin' like a horse in a tin barn in August and there's big splotches of wet on his white shirt. His hair that had been slicked back has started to fall down in his eyes.

I'm beginnin' to feel sorry for Chickie. I think Mr. Dorsey is startin' to feel sorry for us. He looks worried.

The prosecutor says now, Charles, let me

ask you about a couple of other episodes at school.

Chickie gits a worried look on his face and says what?

Do you know Mary Portier?

Chickie looks real worried now. He says yes.

Are you friends?

No, I wouldn't say that.

But you'd like to be friends with Mary, wouldn't you?

I guess.

Joseph and his friends say you spend a lot of time staring at Mary Portier, is that right?

Well, yes sir but lots of boys, uh —

Do you remember earlier this year telling Mary Portier you had found pirate's treasure in your backyard? I think it was treasure from Jean Lafitte, yes?

Uh, well, uh, I don't know if —

Charles, please. Just answer.

Yes sir.

But there was no treasure, was there?

Chickie hangs his head. He says no sir.

And another time did you tell Mary Portier that you had spied a water moccasin crawling under the bleachers where she was sitting?

Uh, well —

In fact you yelled it didn't you?

Uh, well —

And the sole purpose of that was to get Mary to jump up so you could look up her dress, wasn't it?

Chickie's head is hangin' so low at this point I'm afraid it might fall off. Mr. Dorsey says Your Honor, what's the point?

The judge says Mr. Aucoin?

The point, Your Honor, is that Charles Naquin is the kind of person who feels the need to lie at every chance to get attention. And that's just what he's doing in this courtroom today. He's got a personal vendetta against Joseph Guidry and he is lying to hurt Joseph and protect his friend there.

The prosecutor points a long finger at me.

Mr. Dorsey jumps up and says, stern, Your Honor, the prosecutor is preaching not prosecuting.

Chickie half yells I am not! I'm not lyin' about Meely!

The judge raps his gavel again and says hold on a minute, everybody. Mr. Aucoin, be quiet. Mr. Dorsey, please sit down.

He looks stern at poor Chickie and shakes his head and says Mr. Dorsey, I recognize these are serious matters but I'm inclined to side with Mr. Aucoin. This witness has tended to prejudice himself at every opportunity and there are glaring inconsistencies in his testimony. My view is —

Suddenly, there's a voice from the back of the room.

The voice says Your Honor, excuse me. Chickie — I mean, Charles — does tell stories but all those things he's said about Junior and Meely are true.

Every eye in the courtroom turns.

The voice belongs to Joey Hebert.

The next voice is Francis Hebert's. He says son, what the hell do you think you're doin'?

31

The courtroom gits so quiet you could hear a butterfly flappin'. The judge looks annoyed across the courtroom and says young man, who are you and why are you disrupting my courtroom?

Joey says my name is Joey Hebert and I apologize, sir. But I was there. In the boy's room. I heard every word, too, and it was just like Chickie said.

Mr. Hebert pipes up again. He says Your Honor, this boy is my son and I don't think he knows what he's sayin'.

The judge raps hard on the gavel. He looks at Mr. Hebert. He says Francis, is that you?

Mr. Hebert says yes, Your Honor.

He says well, please sit down and be quiet.

He turns to Joey. Now, young Hebert, are you saying that Joseph and his friends said these things in front of you as well?

Well not exactly in front of me. See, I was there but they didn't know it.

The judge says young man, what is it

you're trying to tell me?

Joey looks around and seems suddenly bashful.

He says well, could I tell you in private, Your Honor?

In private?

Yes sir. You see, it's embarrassing and —

The judge glares at Joey. He says young man, what is embarrassing to me is that you are disrupting my courtroom in the middle of a very serious matter. Now, out with it!

Joey looks down and says sorry, Judge. Yes, I heard exactly what Chickie heard. I was, uh, in the stall.

The stall?

Yes, Your Honor. Uh, nature had called.

Mr. Aucoin rises and says Judge, this is absurd. We're bein' blindsided by this witness and —

The judge shakes his head as though he's not shore what to believe. He says pipe down, Mr. Aucoin. He looks long and hard at Joey and takes off his glasses and rubs his temples and then says Mr. Aucoin and Mr. Dorsey, into my chambers. You too, young man. And you, too, Emile.

We go into the judge's office and he shuts the door. He says everybody sit down and we all find chairs.

He says to Joey, young man, are you certain about this?

Yes sir.

Have you had any contact with Mr. Dorsey or Emile here?

Yes sir, with Mr. Dorsey. He asked me to tell what I knew but I said I wouldn't. Or at least that I'd rather not.

And why not? Why didn't you come forward before?

Joey looks at me sheepish like. He says it's no excuse, Your Honor, but Daddy said I shouldn't. He said it wouldn't be wise to be mixed up in LaBauve business.

The judge shakes his head. Son, that's not an excuse. But I'm disappointed in Francis. I know him from the Knights of Columbus. I'm going to have a word with him about this. Now tell me, Joey, did your father know you knew this much about this matter?

No sir. He just knew Mr. Dorsey wanted me to come to court. I didn't tell anyone exactly what I knew except my girlfriend, Claudia.

The judge nods. He says so you understand that what you've done is wrong? Young LaBauve here is in serious trouble. He could go to jail for this. It's important for his sake and for the law's sake to get to the bottom of this.

Yes sir.

And you understand that I could put you under oath and that after Mr. Dorsey questions you, Mr. Aucoin gets a turn to put your feet to the fire?

Yes sir.

And knowing that, this is still your testimony?

Yes sir.

The judge leans back with his hands behind his head and closes his eyes for a second and then rubs his temples again. Then he says Mr. Aucoin, based on what I've heard I'm inclined to grant Mr. Dorsey's motion and release Emile until we figure this out. Furthermore, I want Joseph Guidry and his uncle and those other boys — in fact, all of Joseph Guidry's friends — in my office tomorrow, ten o'clock sharp.

Mr. Aucoin says but Judge, this is not —

No buts, Mr. Aucoin. If this matter goes to trial, and at this point I have my doubts that it will, you will get your crack at young Hebert here. Anyway, I want those boys in here and you tell 'em if they lie to me I'll throw every one of 'em in jail. Do I make myself clear? And I'll do the same to young Hebert here if I find out he's trying to pull a fast one on this court.

The prosecutor says but Judge Petti-bone, we're being asked to take the word of a truant and a colored girl and a self-confessed liar —

The judge says real loud Mr. Aucoin, Emile LaBauve may be a truant but that doesn't automatically make him a criminal. I tend to believe young Hebert here, though it is unfortunate he did not come forward sooner. Charles Naquin is another matter but we now have corroboration of the essence of his story. Coupled with the testimony of Miss Lirette, whom I have no doubt is a woman of great integrity, I think it's highly probable that young LaBauve here may have been a victim of a crime, not the perpetrator. And as for that colored girl, I tend to believe every word she said.

He says to Mr. Dorsey I would like to release Emile immediately but I'm worried about doing so because he is now without parents.

The prosecutor says but Judge, what happens in the event that Chester Cox is found? Emile may be needed as a witness and —

The judge says Mr. Aucoin, you are trying my patience. Please stop.

Mr. Dorsey says Judge, we've thought about Emile's release and Miss Lirette, his teacher, says she would be pleased if Emile would stay with her until something permanent could be worked out. She would even post a bond with the court as a way of assuring Mr. Aucoin that Emile will not leave the parish and will appear when and if he is needed as a witness.

Mr. Dorsey looks at me and says I'm sorry, Your Honor, but I didn't have a chance to discuss this with Emile beforehand. For one thing, I didn't want to raise any false hopes about his getting released.

Judge Pettibone looks at me and says well, young fella, how does that sound?

I feel funny 'cause I know I still have a daddy out there somewhere. But I say Your Honor, I've been in jail for a while now and I've prob'ly had enough of it. I've been over to Miss Lirette's house once and it's nice as she is. If she don't mind, I don't, either.

He says well, it's settled then. Emile you're a free man for now. Don't disappoint me and go running off.

Thank you, Your Honor. I won't.

As for bond, Mr. Dorsey, that's not necessary. If Miss Lirette is prepared to give me her word on the matter, that's good enough for me.

He looks around. Mr. Aucoin ain't happy but he's decided not to say any more about it.

The judge says okay, let's get back in there and get this on the record.

We all walk back into the courtroom. The judge looks at poor Chickie, who's sittin' in the witness chair with his head down. He looks up, fearful, but the judge says in a nice voice it's okay, Charles, you may step down, we're done.

Chickie says you mean I can go?

Yes, for now.

Really?

Really, Charles.

Thank you, Your Honor. I thought for shore I was goin' to the slammer.

The judge smiles for the first time and says Charles, no, not this time. But I wouldn't go yelling to any girls about water moccasins anymore. You'll never get a girlfriend that way.

I don't think it's ever occurred to Chickie that he might git a girlfriend ever.

He says yes sir. I mean, no sir, I won't. Chickie puts up three fingers and says Scout's honor again.

Then the judge tells the court reporter

that court is over till ten o'clock tomorrow morning. He then tells the bailiff who's to come and who doesn't have to. He then tells the bailiff to tell the police that I'm free to go.

The three policemen who've been sittin' in court stare at me and I can tell they're not pleased by what the judge just said. But before we leave, the judge raps his gavel and says one more thing, I have some reason to believe that there might have been police misconduct in this case. Until I get to the bottom of it, I will frown upon any incident involving young LaBauve here and the police. Do you gentlemen back there understand me?

The policemen have all got up. They nod.

Then please have the chief call me so that I can tell him the same thing.

The policemen turn to leave, without sayin' a word.

I turn and see Chickie walkin' out pullin' up his pants and he's so happy to be off the hot seat that he starts practically runnin' for the door.

Joey walks alongside me, lookin' down at the floor. I say thanks, Joey, for standin' up like that.

Joey turns to me and says serious, I'm

sorry, Meely, I shouldn't've listened to Daddy. I should have told what I heard right away.

I say well, Joey, that don't really matter 'cause you said it when it counted.

He says I guess I did. But it wasn't really right to wait.

I say well, that might be true, but I know how it is sometimes with daddies who 'cause trouble.

Joey half smiles at this. He says I guess you would, Meely. Lord, I guess *I'm* in trouble now. Daddy'll ground me for a year.

Just then, I look up to see the judge motionin' to someone. It's Francis Hebert. Mr. Hebert looks at the judge, then looks at me and Joey and turns a bit red. He walks over to the judge and they go into the judge's office and close the door.

I wouldn't care to be Mr. Hebert at this moment. Maybe the judge will git him to go easy on Joey.

We all walk out into the hall and I see Miz Lirette and I go up and thank her. I look for Cassie but she's not there and I figger she's gone back down Catahoula Bayou with her momma. All this commotion has made Miz Jackson nervous.

There's Junior and Uncle and Sergeant

Picou and others in a big knot in the corner, talkin' low. And then Mr. Aucoin comes out and goes over to 'em and he says some words I cain't quite hear and then I hear Junior sayin' real loud well, he's a liar and how can they believe that nigger and that moron Chickie Naquin?

And then I hear Mr. Aucoin say louder, you boys have a lot of explainin' to do to the judge, and you'll be back in here tomorrow to tell the truth or every one of you will go to jail. Every doggone one of you! And if you're not here I will personally send the police to get you. You especially, Junior Guidry. And it won't be your uncle I'm sendin', you understand me?

The talk suddenly goes out of that whole bunch.

Then I walk out with Mr. Dorsey and Miz Lirette and the others into the sunshine and it feels good to be free.

And I think, Junior won't ever give up. Ever.

But Miz Jackson's right when she once said Junior ain't got a lick of sense.

That boy is several shrimp short of a gumbo.

32

It's October now and the cool weather has moved in and it's the nicest time of the year to be livin' on Catahoula Bayou. The sky is deep blue and the cane's head high and there was frost on the ground two days ago. They'll start cuttin' and grindin' the cane soon.

Squirrel season's open and I go on the weekends, me and Rascal. He's a half-growed beagle Miz Lirette give me when I moved in. She says a boy should have a dog, which is fine by me. Rascal's young yet and full of mischief and will be better at rabbits than squirrels but that's okay. We go out and ramble around the woods and always git us a few.

Joey comes along when he ain't got too much else to do. His daddy talks to me regular now. Joey says the judge give Mr. Hebert an earful and though Mr. Hebert was still plenty mad he ain't cut Joey out of that will yet.

I still ain't been to supper in that big house, though.

Miz Lirette don't eat squirrel nor does her sister, Eugenia, who's nice but real quiet. But they don't mind if I fry up the young 'uns or make stew out of the ole ones. Miz Lirette says Meely, I cain't believe you crack those heads open and eat the brains and I say that's the best part, Miz Lirette. It might be a Wild Injun thing, since Daddy taught me to do it.

She does eat my *sauce piquante*, though, as does Eugenia. She's tickled that I cook.

I'm in school all the time now. They put me back in eighth grade, which is behind where I should be but not all that bad considerin' how much I didn't go. I'm small, anyways, so I don't look that out of place. But it's funny. Last year I was one year ahead of Joey and now I'm one year behind. It don't really matter, though. My teacher, Mr. Brien, is strict and not as friendly as Miz Lirette. But he says I'm doin' real good and Miz Lirette helps me if I'm stuck on homework. I cain't say I'm fond of homework but I don't mind it as much as I thought I might.

I'm better at figgerin' than I thought I would be, too. I might even try algebra one day, though I still don't know what I'd ever use it for.

Junior quit school after all the trouble,

which I'm glad for. He's still around and workin' for his daddy but Miz Lirette says Junior ain't gonna bother me no more 'cause he himself almost got put in the reform school he was hopin' I'd git sent to. She says the judge told him if he ever comes after me again he *will* go to reform school.

Maybe that has impressed Junior. I kinda doubt it myself. I'm still plannin' to stay clear of him.

Ole Chickie found out somethin' else pretty interestin'. He says them red aints Chilly dumped down Junior's pants bit Junior so bad that his pecker swelled up big as a watermelon and he was in a bad way for days. I axed Joey and he says he heard a cantaloupe.

Either way, Chilly would be tickled. Daddy, too.

As for the rest, Mr. Dorsey says Roddy and those boys went before the judge and all told the truth and Uncle just about got fired. He says Uncle works on the desk now pushin' a pencil and is no longer a sergeant but somethin' a lot lower. He says they shoulda prosecuted him or at least got rid of him, Meely, but that's politics for you. He says the Guidrys got so much family around that the police chief that hired Uncle cain't easily fire him lest all the Guidrys vote for another chief.

I don't know what politics really is, but I cain't say I'm for it if it let Uncle off easy.

I saw Cassie once right after I got out of jail. Miz Lirette lets me go where I want to so long as I tell her I'm goin' and when more or less I'm comin' back. She says that way, Meely, if you're bit by a snake I'll know where to send out the posse to find you.

She smiles when she says this 'cause she knows how I feel about the chance of a posse findin' anybody. But I think Miz Lirette worries about me a bit, which I guess I don't mind. She likes it when I git home before dark if I've gone fishin' or huntin', but she leaves on the porch light just in case.

I've got my own big room in her big ole house and even a feather mattress on my bed.

Daddy would be tickled by that.

I've got my own closet and a chest of drawers. Miz Lirette bought me a nice new frame for that pitcher of Momma and me and it sits atop the dresser.

The day I went to see Cassie I told Miz Lirette I was goin' fishin' up at the Perch Hole. She offered to drive me but I said I like to walk, which I do. I did take my pole and some worms. But instead I walked over and knocked on Miz Jackson's door. Only Cassie was there.

She looked real good and smiled bright when she saw me and said she was glad all that trouble with Junior and Uncle was over.

I said me too.

She said Meely, I wish I knew more 'bout what happened to your daddy. All I know is that he and Chilly got out of the swamp and on the highway to New Awlins and got a ride with a colored farmer goin' up to Tupelo. Chilly's got kin up there. He says he tried to git your daddy to stay but your daddy said he had to git back down to check on some things. That's the last he saw of him.

I felt bad that I couldn't tell Cassie that I thought Daddy was alive someplace. But I just couldn't. So I said well, Cassie, things happen.

Well, it's too bad that things like that do.

I said yes that's true.

She said I'm goin' up to see Chilly on the Trailways bus.

I said well, tell him hello for me.

She said Chilly was my boyfriend and I got mad at him but after that business with

Junior and Uncle I couldn't stay mad no more. I miss him a whole lot and we write letters to each other. She said his momma and my momma have knowed each other forever.

I said that's real nice.

I was tempted to say that her momma and my momma knowed each other pretty good too but I didn't. I didn't think it would git me anywhere near heaven again.

She said Chilly cain't never come back here, so I might not either.

I said well, now that Roddy and that gang said the truth maybe he could.

She said shuh, Meely, they'd still have it in for him. He'd always be watchin' his backsides. It's different for us colored people, you know.

I said it's kinda different for us Wild Injuns, too.

Cassie laughed at that. She said you're a sweet boy, Meely, and we had us a time, for shore, but we couldn't be steady me and you.

I said I s'pected we couldn't.

She said the world still don't understand black and white.

I said there's lots the world don't understand, that's for shore.

She said some ole girl will be lucky one day.

I didn't know what to say to that. So we stood silent for a long while. Then she said well, good-bye, Meely. I won't forgit you. Ever.

I said I won't forgit you either.

Cassie kissed me soft on the lips and I left.

It was my first real kiss. Seems a shame to git it that way.

I think about Cassie a lot. Sometimes I wonder whether what happened between us ever really happened. It all seems so dreamy and long ago.

Sometimes I think about goin' over to see Miz Jackson but I ain't yet.

But I s'pect I will when things feel a little different.

33

It's Saturday late mornin' and me and Rascal have come in from squirrel huntin'. I got my limit of ten. I hunted a new place that Miz Lirette's ole uncle told me about and it was loaded with big fox squirrels.

It was a perfect mornin', still and foggy. On such a mornin' a squirrel cain't hide easily as everyplace he goes he shakes water off the trees. Daddy says a good squirrel hunter hunts with his ears as much as his eyes.

There's a note for me on the kitchen table from Miz Lirette sayin' she and Eugenia have gone to town to the hardware store. I know what for — mousetraps.

I feed Rascal then go to the kitchen and make coffee and pour a cup and go out and sit on the back porch in Miz Eugenia's big green rockin' chair. I like that chair. It's got a rope back and a cushioned seat and big arms. I'll have some coffee then skin my squirrels.

I sit in the rocker and Rascal curls up at my feet. He's worked hard this mornin'.

He ran all over creation chasin' rabbits and he even treed two squirrels.

The fog has burned off leavin' only blue sky. It's got nice and warm after a chilly start. Daddy calls these days Injun summer though I'm not shore why.

From our back porch sugarcane waves far as the eye can see. They'll cut this stand soon and we'll have a view of the woods way distant. And the field mice will come in and invade the house and Miz Lirette and Miz Eugenia will have fits.

They've already told me they hate those mice and they have axed me if I know how to git rid of 'em.

I said well, in my house durin' harvest I used to take my BB gun and lay behind a pillow in the hall leadin' to the kitchen. I'd turn off all the lights 'cept the kitchen light and put cheese on the floor and when them mice would come I'd pick 'em off one by one.

One night I shot fourteen, which is my record.

Miz Lirette laughed at that and said Meely, I think I'll buy me some mouse-traps.

I hear a rustle in the cane off the end of the porch and Rascal gives a little bark. I say hush, Rascal.

A man walks out of the field.

It's Daddy.

He says hello, Meely.

I say hello, Daddy.

He says that shore is a nice mess of squirrels you got.

I say I got my limit — every one a fox squirrel.

He says well, you're prob'ly a better squirrel hunter than me now.

I say I doubt that, Daddy.

He says boy, it's a beautiful day for squirrel huntin'.

I say it don't git no better.

Daddy looks up at the clear blue sky. Then he says that's one good-lookin' beagle you got there.

I say his name is Rascal and he's a good dog, for shore.

Daddy pats his leg. C'mere, pup.

Rascal goes over and nuzzles Daddy's hand.

I say Miz Lirette give me that dog.

Daddy says I'd say it looks like she picked a good 'un.

A little Injun summer breeze blows and Daddy looks up again and puts up a hand to shield his eyes from the sun.

I say Daddy, are you all right?

He says fit as a fiddle.

How'd you know I was here?

I didn't really. I snuck by the ole house and saw it was all boarded up. So I decided I might come and ax Miz Lirette about you. I figger she'd be the only one who would tell me and not call in the police. I was ducked out of sight in the field when I saw you come in with your squirrels.

I say well, you're right, Miz Lirette wouldn't call the police. Anyway the police ain't really lookin' for you no more.

Daddy looks at me funny. He says why on earth not, son?

I say 'cause you're dead.

I'm dead?

Yes sir. A gator drowned you. Or else you drowned, then gators and crawfish ate you up.

Daddy shakes his head. He says you've got me puzzled, son.

I tell him the story of the man in the hospital and the funeral and all.

Daddy says Meely, now I've heard everything. Where am I buried?

In the Catahoula Cemetery.

Not next to your momma, I hope?

No sir. Over by the back fence.

Well, Meely, I'll be dog. Is my name on the tomb and everything?

I say it is. Logan LaBauve. I would've had 'em put your middle name but I didn't know it.

It's Earl.

Okay, Daddy. Next time I'll know.

Daddy shakes his head and grins. He says that beats all I ever heard, Meely. You shore was thinkin' on your feet again. Did they keep you long in jail?

Long enough to know I didn't care for it. I can see why you give up on jail, Daddy.

I'm sorry you had it so rough.

I say not so rough 'cept for nasty Sergeant Picou. Anyway, Judge Pettibone really roughed up Junior and Roddy and that bunch and even Uncle, and I got let out for good.

Daddy says I s'pose that makes for one honest judge. It's good to know there might be one.

I say I reckon it does.

Daddy goes quiet like he's thinkin' all this over. He says well, are they treatin' you right here?

I say it's pretty comfortable. I would've stayed at the ole house 'cept they threatened to put me in an orphanage, plus they boarded it all up. I go down there sometimes and sit on the back porch.

Shuh, Meely, it's better here. That ole

house is gonna fall down soon anyways.

I tell Daddy about my room and my feather mattress.

He says I'll be dog, Meely.

I tell Daddy that I don't mind school now and I go regular and might even take algebra one day.

He says well, Meely, you've got your momma's book smarts, that's for shore. That's really good, son. I might have a better opinion of school if they start treatin' you right.

I say so far they are, Daddy.

Things git quiet for a while and finally Daddy says well, just 'cause I'm dead don't mean they won't git after me if they know I'm not.

I say that's true. Mr. Dorsey, the one who was my lawyer, says they prob'ly couldn't prove much 'cept how you took your truck back and shot up the police car. But they still might throw you in jail for that.

Shuh, Meely, I guess I shouldn't've shot up that car.

I say maybe not, Daddy. But in a way I'm glad you did. I'm glad Chilly put red aints down their pants, too.

I tell Daddy about Junior's watermelon problem.

Daddy laughs so hard at this that I think he's gonna fall down. I haven't seen Daddy laugh such in a long time.

He says you know Chilly got away?

I say I knew. Cassie told me.

Daddy says I gotta say we had ourselves a pretty good time in that swamp everything considered.

I bet you did.

They never come close to catchin' us 'cept once. Heck, Meely, they sent a durned hellycopter after us.

They did?

They shore did, son. Lucky we heard it comin' and paddled under some cypress trees.

I say well, 'cordin' to Sergeant Picou, they had the entire U.S. Army lookin' for you.

Daddy laughs and says I bet they did. Anyway, Chilly wanted me to stay up there in Mississippi but I had to git back down.

How come?

Well I figgered if you stayed to tell our side I should come back to see how you was makin' out.

I say I 'preciate that, Daddy.

He says I don't know what I'd've done if you were still in jail, Meely. I'm pretty good at gittin' into jail but I'm not so shore about the bustin' out part.

I say ain't that the truth.

Daddy laughs. He says well, Meely, you 'member that man in Florda who used to come down and buy little live gators from me?

I do.

Well, he once told me LaBauve, if you ever wanna come down and help me run my gator farm I could use a man like you. Ain't nobody down there knows gators like you.

I s'pect not, Daddy.

Daddy says I called him c'lect while I was up in Mississippi and he says I can still come. I don't think the police would come that far to git me, even if they knowed I was alive. His farm is way back in a swamp, anyways. My kind of place.

I say Daddy, Mr. Dorsey says the arm of the law is long and the law don't ever forgit. So I just think we should leave you dead.

Daddy says that's prob'ly best, son. It's a long way down there but I should be able to hitch.

I say well, be careful of the police till you git out of Loosiana. Maybe you should sneak up to the New Awlins road and flag the Greyhound. Stay off the highways.

I would, Meely, 'cept money's a little tight. I about give the pirogue away to some ole trapper for five dollars and I sold one gator hide up in Mississippi. I've been pretty much shootin' all my food.

I think about this for a second then remember somethin'. I say Daddy, you just wait a minute.

I turn and go in through the back screen door and to my room. I kneel down and fetch a tin can from under my bed.

I open it and take out Velma's thirty-five dollars, which Junior and Uncle hadn't found after all. I put the can away and go back out on the porch.

I say take this and catch that bus.

Daddy takes the money and looks at it puzzled.

I say there's thirty-five dollars there.

He says boy, Meely, that's a lot of money. You musta worked hard at somethin' for this.

I say I didn't have to, Daddy. It's actually your money — it's the money you give Velma that night she come over and burnt up the mattress. She give it to me and said to save it for a rainy day.

I look up at the clear sky and say this ain't a rainy day but it's a good day to use the money.

Daddy shakes his head again. He says well, good ole Velma. If I ever see her again I'm liable to kiss her.

I say I s'pect you might, Daddy. She'd prob'ly let you if you give her thirty-five dollars again.

Daddy laughs hard and it's nice to see Daddy laugh such. Then he says you shore you don't wanna keep it, Meely?

Daddy, I wouldn't know how to spend that much money plus Miz Lirette gives me a little each week for helpin' out, which I do.

Well, okay, son.

We go quiet. In a while I ax Daddy if he wants some coffee. I don't s'pect Miz Lirette back till much later. Daddy says he shore wouldn't mind a cup. I go in and pour it and bring it out and Daddy says this is the best coffee I've had since I run away. He drinks it slow and looks around and says boy, Meely, this shore is a nice place they've got here.

It shore is, Daddy.

He says well, after I git to Florda and git settled I'll send you a bus ticket. That ole boy down there says there's beaches white as sugar and the ocean's as blue as the sky.

I say no foolin'? I shore wouldn't mind seein' that one day.

Daddy hands me the cup and says well, Meely, you and that dog take care of yourselves. I better be gittin'.

We will, Daddy. You, too.

Daddy smiles and turns and then turns again. He comes over and gives me a hug, first one I've had from Daddy since I don't know when.

Then he disappears, quiet as a rabbit, into the cane field.

34

Daddy's been gone more than a week. The weather is still nice. It's dinnertime up at school and I eat my dirty rice and peas with Joey and then excuse myself and go outside to sit in the sun. I walk over to the softball field, thinkin' I might perch on the bleachers. I look up.

There's Mary Portier, sittin' up on top.

Improper.

She's readin' a book and has on yellow ones today. It's funny how I feel, all goosey.

I remember how she acted at Daddy's funeral and how nice she smelled and all the nice things she said to me.

Just as I think how I shouldn't be starin', she lowers the book and sees me.

Meely LaBauve, whatever are you doin'?

I'm suddenly flustered and I feel my face git hot as a welder's torch. I say, uh, nothin'.

She crosses her legs, though not in a big hurry or anything, and smooths her dress.

Hhm, is that right? You were just standin' there?

I guess I've turned pretty red by now.

I shrug and say oh well, I was lookin' around is all.

She says lookin' around huh? Did you see anything interestin'?

I say uh, the sky's pretty. It's Injun summer you know.

She says yes, I know all about Indian summer. So it was the sky? You were lookin' up at the sky, Meely?

Uh, yeah, I was.

I shuffle my feet some.

She says and what color was the sky?

What color?

Yeah, what color — was it yellow, Meely?

My face is a regular fire truck by now. I cain't look directly at Mary but she says wanna come up here and sit next to me?

I look up. Mary has her arms folded and she's lookin' serious but I can tell she's not really. I say okay.

I climb up the bleachers and settle in next to Mary. She smiles and I git goosey again.

She says why are boys all terrible, can you tell me that?

I don't know what to say, so I shrug.

She says it's not polite to try to look up a girl's dress.

I say sorry, I guess it's not.

She says I'll forgive you this time, Meely, 'cause you don't know any better and you've had such a hard time. If you were Chickie Naquin I'd've thrown my book at you.

I say well, I'm awful glad I'm not him.

She laughs at this and says he's *such* a brat, Meely.

I say he can be that.

She says but it's nice the way you try to stick up for him sometimes. Everybody needs a friend.

I say well, Daddy always says the measure of a big dog ain't that he can bite the little ones.

She laughs again and says that's a good way to put it, Meely. Then she gits serious again and says are you okay?

I say shore, don't I look it?

She says silly boy, you know what I mean. All the trouble you've been through. It's all got to be quite a shock. Junior and his gang picking on you so and all that trouble with the police. Plus your poor daddy. I don't know what I'd do if I lost my parents. I think it's just all awful and I think you must be very brave the way you've handled it all.

I look at Mary and see how soft and blue her eyes are. I realize I don't mind that she feels bad for me. I don't mind that she thinks I've handled it all very well.

Mary says you'll have to tell me all about it sometime. That is, if you want to, Meely. I know it's hard, but if you ever want to talk about it you can talk to me.

I realize how little I've ever talked to girls, 'cept Cassie, about anything. So I shrug and say Mary, sometime that might be real nice.

She says I'll bet you miss your daddy, Meely.

I think about this and realize it's not a lie to say that I do. Daddy's barely been gone but who knows when I'll see him again.

I say I do miss him, Mary. Daddy was a bit of trouble but he was one of a kind, that's for shore.

She says, I'm sure he's gone to a better place. We've just got to believe that, Meely. She reaches over and touches my arm when she says this.

I almost smile at this 'cause Mary's got a lot closer to the truth than she thinks. I'm imaginin' Daddy down there in Florda workin' on that gator farm. I imagine him on a sugar-sand beach where the ocean is as blue as the sky. Maybe he's rompin' around with somebody like Velma with a good bottle of somethin' or other.

Some people die and go to heaven. Maybe Daddy has lived and gone there.

Then the bell rings and me and Mary walk down off the bleachers. I see Joey and Claudia Toups have come out to sit on the grass and they git up and walk with us. Then I see Chickie and he comes by and looks us all over funny like and says, Meely, did you shoot you any squirrels today? Then he skips ahead cacklin' like a *poule d'eau.*

Mary looks at me funny for a second and then *she* turns red and says did he mean what I think he meant?

Poor Chickie. I can see he's about to git in trouble again so I say to Mary well, you know Chickie, he don't always talk sense.

And Mary looks around and, seein' that Chickie is gone and Joey and Claudia have walked ahead of us, suddenly takes me by the arm and looks into my eyes and says real low with a smile that just about kills me well, Meely LaBauve, *he* should be so lucky.

GLOSSARY OF CAJUN TERMS

Cajun — a shortening of the term Acadian and referring to eighteenth-century refugees of French extraction who were exiled to Louisiana from Canada's Acadia Province by the British during the French and Indian War; more broadly, South Louisiana residents of various ethnic backgrounds who have adopted Cajun speech, customs, and food as their own.

chaoui (sha-WEE) — raccoon.

choupique (shoe-PICK) — alternate spelling, *tchoupique;* mud-fish, bowfin, grunnion. Also the cypress trout.

cochon de lait (co-SHOHN duh lay) — literally, suckling pig; in many places, a social gathering centered around the roasting of a freshly slaughtered pig.

couillon (coo-YOHN) — nut; funny, in a crazy way.

étouffée (ay-too-FAY) — a stew of brown

gravy, usually made with seafood, typically crawfish and shrimp.

fâché (fah-SHAY) — upset; angry.

fais dodo (FAY doe-doe) — informal title of a popular Cajun lullaby; also, a country dance.

flottant (flo-TOHN) — in French, "floating" or "buoyant"; in Cajun a floating marsh.

gris-gris (gree-gree) — a spell or charm; a curse.

gumbo — a soup, usually of chicken, sausage, seafood, or okra or a combination of the above, made with a roux and served in bowls over rice.

Jolie blonde, 'gardez donc quoi t'as fait/tu m'as quitte' pour t'en aller — Pretty blonde, so look what you did/you left me to go . . .

maudit fils de garce, fils de putain, chu de cochon — Mean bastard, son of a bitch, pig's ass.

nègre (*neg*) — used by Cajuns as a term of endearment, as in *"mon nègre,"* meaning "my dear little boy."

pirogue (PEE-row; alternately pee-rog) — the Cajun equivalent of a canoe.

poule d'eau (pool doo) — coot; literally, water chicken.

pop rouge — strawberry soda.

réveiller, cher 'tit chou — wake up, my dear little sweetheart.

roux (roo) — flour browned in oil or lard and used as the base for gumbos, étouffées, and other Cajun dishes.

sac-à-lait (sock-oh-LAY) — a panfish, specifically a crappie.

sauce piquante (sauce pee-KOHNT) — a spicy tomato stew, usually made with rabbit or chicken.

traînasse (trehn-OSS) — a boat trail through the marsh, usually man-made.

Zatarain's — a popular, commercially available seasoning mixture used in boiling crabs, shrimp, or crawfish.

The author acknowledges as his primary source for these definitions *A Dictionary of the Cajun Language* by the Reverend Jules O. Daigle, published in 1984 by Edwards Brothers, Ann Arbor, Michigan.

A GUIDE TO

PRONOUNCING CAJUN NAMES

Arceneaux (ARE-sin-oh)
Ardoin (ARE-dwehn)
Aucoin (Oh-kwehn)
Bergeron (Bear-zher-rohn)
Bonvillain (BON-vee-lehn)
Breaux (Bro)
Cancienne (KAHN-see-ehn)
Comeaux (Como)
Daigle (Deg; alternately DAY-gull)
Giroir (Zhih-wah)
Guidry (Gid-dree)
Hebert (A-bear)
Landry (Land-dree)
LaBauve (Le-bove, rhymes with cove)
Lirette (Lee-rette)
Naquin (Knock-ehn)
Sevin (SAY-vehn)
Schexnayder (SHECKS-ny-der)
Picou (Pee-coo)
Portier (Por-chay)
Trahan (Trah-hahn)

ABOUT THE AUTHOR

Ken Wells grew up on the banks of Bayou Black, deep in Louisiana's Cajun belt. He got his first newspaper job as a nineteen-year-old college dropout, covering car wrecks and gator sightings for *The Courier*, the Houma, Louisiana, weekly newspaper, while still helping out in his family's snake-collecting business. He is now a senior writer and features editor for *The Wall Street Journal*'s Page One staff. He lives with his family on the outskirts of Manhattan.

Meely LaBauve is his first novel.